EMPOWERED

THE POWER SERIES: BOOK TWO

VICTORIA WOODS

EMPOWERED

First Edition. March 22, 2021.

TABLE OF CONTENTS

Playlist

Power by Kanye West

Again by Lennie Kravitz

Gangsta by Kehlani

Genius by LSD ft. Sia, Diplo and Labrinth

Dhol, Dark & Handsome by DJ Rekha

Toxic by Alex & Sierra

Bed by J. Holiday

Motivation by Kelly Rowland ft. Lil Wayne

Beggin' by Madcon

Meri Jaan by Juggy D ft. Jay Sean

Get Me by Justin Bieber ft. Kehlani

Don't Speak by No Doubt

Yesterday by The Beatles

Fly by Nicki Minaj & Rihanna

Supermarket Flowers by Ed Sheeran

Scan the code below to listen in the SEARCH bar of your Spotify account to listen along!

TRIGGER WARNING

Subject matters like rape and abuse that may be dark and disturbing to some readers is included in this book

Chapter I

Shyam

Thick red hair flowed freely around my face as soft supple lips kneaded mine. They compelled me to match their pace—slow and steady—even though I wanted to consume them fully. The smooth tongue driving me wild teased my own into seeking another taste. I drew in the breaths that were fed to me, inhaling them deep down into my chest—absorbing them into my soul.

The lips that I coveted pulled out of reach too soon, leaving me yearning for more. They moved to my jaw, skimming gently over my stubble. Soft kisses diffused across my chest as beautiful petals of hair trailed lower, tickling my face as they drifted further down my body.

Smooth thighs hugged my pelvis taunting me as lush lower lips rubbed along my length. The bouquet of red hair on my chest parted, revealing the face of the angel smiling down at me.

"Amelia," I whispered, smoothing my thumb across her fair cheek. Her green eyes shone with the same adoration that had just rolled off my tongue in her whispered name.

Her radiant body stayed upright, displaying her nymph-like features. The light streaming from the windows highlighted her round breasts sprinkled with delicate freckles. Pink nipples stood at their peaks, tempting me to taste them.

Silky sheets caressed my skin as she lifted her hips up, taking me inside of her, squeezing me with her tightness. Moans escaped from my throat as she rocked on top of me with long and lazy strokes. I thickened inside of her, chasing my glorious release.

Our hands found each other's, our fingers intertwining as we fell over the cliff together. Her forehead pressed against mine as we took our last steadying breaths to settle the waves of emotion that we shared.

My hands held her face closed to mine. "Amelia," I whispered. She pulled away slowly, not saying anything in return. "Amelia," I called out again, hoping she would come back to me. The warmth of her body left my frame, leaving me cold and hollow. "Amelia!" I cried out louder, commanding her to return to me. She ignored my demand, moving farther away from the bed. I tried to force my arms and legs to move to retrieve her. My limbs wouldn't listen to the nerve impulses fired by my brain. Paralysis left me frozen to the mattress. I screamed for her to come back to me. "Amelia!"

I jolted awake from my dream. My nightmare.

My senses returned and I was aware of the hell that I had returned to. The room was dark even though it was probably after noon. Time was irrelevant in perdition. Torment had no limit here.

Empty scotch glasses lined my bedside table. The sheets were damp from the cold sweat that had overtaken my body, but I didn't get up to change them. Nothing mattered anymore. I was numb inside, all motivation gone.

The days had blurred into each other after I received Amelia's necklace from my enemy. I called off the search for her because the evidence of her death had shone back at me in my own hands.

I lay buck naked in bed, the precum from my wet-dream-turned-nightmare drying into a sticky mess on my dick. I was exhausted from the hurricane of emotions that churned inside of me and I didn't want to *feel* anymore. I just wanted to sleep it all away. However, my brief reprieve was always ruined by the same nightmare. The very one I had just had. And when I couldn't sleep, I just lay in my bed, replaying memories of her.

Tarun didn't kill her. I did. And I deserved the guilt that consumed my soul.

A knock sounded at my bedroom door. I didn't bother answering it. It could only be one of two people, my maid, or my brother. If I ignored them long enough, they would hopefully go away.

"Hey." I could see Jai leaning against the doorframe from my periphery, but I didn't acknowledge him. "I know it's late, but I brought you breakfast. Or, rather, that shit you normally *call* breakfast. Salmon with some sort of tasteless weeds grown by Icelandic orphans in an organic meadow, or something or other."

I didn't respond.

He continued, "Yeah, that doesn't sound tempting to me either. Let's hit up the bar for some scotch and cigars? My treat."

He sighed, exasperated from effort he was putting in. "Look, I've been trying to be supportive and sensitive, but this kid-glove, gentle bullshit isn't my thing."

This time, I answered. "Go fuck yourself," I muttered. I didn't want his pity. I just wanted him to leave me the hell alone.

His image grew larger as he got closer to the bed. He yanked the pillow out from under my head, causing my head to drop directly onto the mattress. He slammed it onto my head, behaving just like the annoying little brother he was. I pushed the pillow to the side to uncover my face.

4

"Get the fuck up. This isn't like you, man. I get that you're heartbroken. I'm torn up about Amelia, too. But her body is still out there. You owe it to her to give her the proper burial she deserves and kill that motherfucker for what he took from you."

Reluctantly, I sat up against the headboard, using the last bit of energy I had stored away. My head swam from getting up too fast. I hadn't been upright in so long that my balance was off. "You don't think I know that? You don't think that I curse myself every minute for getting her involved? You don't think that I want Tarun six feet underground for fucking with me?"

"Then what the fuck is stopping you? Man up. Get up out of this pigsty," he said kicking a pile of clothes on the floor. "Salena is still alive. We can at least save one life. Do it for Mom. Do it for Amelia. If you really loved her, then get your ass up."

I had never discussed my true feelings for Amelia with anyone, but hearing Jai talk about them stung deep inside of my chest—so bad that my breath stopped for a moment. Tears blurred my vision, threatening to fall.

My brother realized he had achieved what he needed to—shaking me out of my half-dead state to get a reaction. Satisfied, he softened his approach and took a seat at the edge of the bed. His voice was gentle and full of sympathy as he witnessed my torture. "Shyam, you have to do this. We need to finish this."

"I know," I said solemnly, diverting my eyes from his. He was right. Staying in bed and mourning was just giving Tarun license to take more of what was mine.

"You won't be alone. You'll have me by your side." He put his hand on my shoulder. I knew he'd always have my back. But he also needed me to have his, too. This was *our* business and although he never said it, he depended on me just as much as I did on him. I couldn't let him down. He was the only family I had.

CHAPTER II

AMELIA

I wished sleep would come easily in my cell, but it never did. The mattress on the floor was hard and uncomfortable. The cement floor beneath it was even worse. There wasn't much in the way of furniture— just a bench bolted to the wall. There were no windows either, so I could only tell the time of day by the presence of sunlight through the skylight above the hallway in front of my cell. At night, the skylight was dark, triggering the lights in the hallway to turn on.

I didn't even have a toilet, just a hole in the ground where I had to squat to pee. I tried hard to hold it if I could, until my bladder was painfully full.

I heard keys jangling, which meant a guard was approaching. They usually stopped by twice a day with a bowl full of unidentifiable mush they called a "meal." I had held out for the first few offerings, skeptical of what the slop was laced with. However, my stomach had eventually gotten the best of me. It was even more putrid than it looked, but my belly had begged for something to fill it, so I managed to swallow it down. That first time, I'd had to squeeze my nostrils shut with my fingers to swallow whole without chewing to avoid tasting it. I needed every bit of strength I could get if I were ever going to break out of here.

This time, the guard didn't come to my cell. Instead, he dragged a tall woman with long brown hair behind him. She didn't resist his handling and followed behind him without making a sound, like she was used to this. He opened the gate to the cell directly across from mine and despite his prisoner's cooperation, he shoved her inside like she was trash before locking the gate and walking away.

I studied the woman who lay glued to the cement floor. I noticed she didn't wear cuffs around her wrists like I did, probably because they knew she would never try to fight back. She wore traditional Indian wear made of cotton—loose pants with a dress-like tunic that fell to knee-length. The colors were vibrant and very unfitting of a woman who was supposed to be a captive. But then again, what did I know about the formalities of being a captive? Hell, I was dressed in a skimpy red evening gown, or whatever remained of it after all the rips.

Her curtain of shiny hair blocked her face so I couldn't make out her features. She was too thin, like she needed a good meal, and her skin was marred with dark bruises. They were a stark contrast to the beautiful henna that was sprawled over her hands and forearms. These men must really be monsters if they would hurt a person who seemed as compliant as her.

I rose from my mattress and walked closer to the bars on my cell. "Hey, are you okay?" I asked.

The woman looked up at me, her eyes wide from fear.

I tried to calm her down. "It's okay. I just wanted to see if they hurt you."

She backed away to the far wall of her cell. More of her hair shifted out of her face and I got a better view of her familiar features.

"Salena," I gasped. I was sure it was her. She looked just like her photo, beautiful yet robbed of the life in her eyes. Except now, those eyes were filled with terror.

"Salena!" I called out louder. She huddled against the wall like a cornered animal, turning her face away to avoid me.

"I'm Amelia. I'm a friend of Shyam's." I hadn't uttered his name aloud in so long that it felt like a prayer on my lips when

I said it. Salena seemed to have the same reaction at hearing her ex-fiancé's name, staring off in a daze.

"Shyam?" she repeated back in disbelief.

Another nearby guard must have overheard us because he stalked over to my cell with a murderous expression and opened the gate with a murderous expression. "You want to talk, bitch? I'll teach you to talk," he spat as he neared me.

"I'm sorry." I threw my hands up in surrender. "Please don't hurt me."

I tried to retreat deeper into my cell, but he grabbed me by the throat and threw me to the ground. My head slammed against the concrete. His foot smashed into my stomach, forcing the wind out of me. Black dots freckled my vision.

My hands instinctively moved to my stomach to protect myself from another blow. I didn't anticipate the fat fingers that grabbed me by my hair. He pushed his face up close to mine as I gasped for breath. He was missing teeth and tattoos covered his face. "Keep your mouth shut, you cunt." He threw me back down onto the ground, causing my face to hit the cement with blinding force. The metallic tang of blood coated my mouth. I stayed frozen, face down, until I heard his footsteps fade.

Before he left the hallway, I heard him threaten Salena. "You're lucky you're marrying the boss; else you'd get the same."

He banged on the gates of her cell to reinforce his point. She let out a yelp that sounded more like the squeak of a mouse.

She had clearly been the victim of abuse, but maybe it wasn't all from the guards. I was betting her *future husband* was a participant.

I listened for the guard's steps to disappear before rolling over onto my back, then I let the tears that I had been holding in release. I prayed for the strength to recover from the blows I had been dealt. I prayed that one day I would see Shyam's face again. And finally, I prayed that I would survive another night in this hell.

CHAPTER III

SHYAM

It was torturous to get out of bed and dress myself this morning. My body was still hard with muscle but the days of drinking scotch and lying sedentary had caused me to lose some mass, making my suit fit looser. Dark circles encased my eyes, and my skin lacked its usual tan color since I was so dehydrated from all the liquor consumption. I didn't even bother grooming the stubble that had taken over my jaw.

Luckily, Sethi Tech had remained intact during my absence. We had competent employees who could carry on regardless of management presence, but it was rare that I was ever out of the office for days on end. At least I could count on Jai to be there. He had stepped up and taken over the reins while I had been licking my wounds at home like an injured dog. Despite his reckless tendencies, I knew I could depend on him.

I stepped out of the elevator and onto my floor. The building was quieter than usual since most people were away on holiday vacation. A couple of lingering board members who were there tying up loose-ends stopped me to bid pleasantries. I wasn't in the mood to make small talk, so I cut the conversations short and headed to my office. Though, I had the nagging urge to make a pitstop first. I wandered past the fountain and maze of glass sculptures that we had paid an arm for.

I reached the closed door of my destination. I knew I shouldn't look, but it was like a car crash that I couldn't ignore. Turning the door handle, I moved inside and flicked the light switch on.

Amelia's office. Everything looked as it had before she was taken, except she wasn't there. The office still smelled fresh, like she had just been sitting behind her desk, nose buried behind her monitor, typing furiously. The ache in my chest, which was always with me like an old friend, now turned into a piercing pain. I closed my eyes and rested my head against the doorway, needing deep breaths to steady myself. When would this guilt ever go away?

Shutting the door, I locked the ghosts of the past inside. My focus now was to get her body back here to give her the proper burial she deserved. Funeral rites were important in my culture because we believed they were needed for a person's soul to be at peace and to move on to the next life. Amelia and I hadn't ever discussed religion or her beliefs about the afterworld. However, Amelia's mother deserved to bury her child and mourn her loss. I had decided on waiting to break the news to her mother until we found her body. It would be easier on her that way, rather than causing her more heartbreak over her daughter's missing body.

The office wasn't the place to have a breakdown, so I kept walking and shut my grief into a tightly closed compartment.

Jai was already waiting inside of my office. "Hey," he said patiently seated across from my desk.

"Hey," I said, unbuttoning my jacket before sitting down. "You're here early." I cocked an eyebrow unable to hide my surprise.

He smirked. "Oh, you know. I've gotta keep these developers in line."

Ignoring his attempt to lighten my mood, I placed my hands on my desk, ready to get to work. "What did I miss?"

We spent the whole morning discussing how Tarun's network of distributors had grown even more. More of our shipments had been destroyed during transit. Many of the distributors that remained with us were furious. Jai tried to appease them, but since we couldn't deliver our product successfully, they eventually defected to Tarun's side. We were losing millions of dollars at an astounding rate.

Nearly one hundred of our men had been moved undercover to Jaipur to search for Tarun. They had been questioning people to find out if they had seen someone who looked like him or Amelia. She would have easily stood out with her red hair, European features, and American accent. The men were careful so as not to raise suspicion, but the trail was cold.

Our most trusted man, Zayn, was overseeing the search. He had been by our side since we were kids. His father had worked for ours, so we grew up together, and I knew I could trust him.

Zayn had updated Jai daily while I was gone. He also knew what Salena looked like, so he kept his eyes open for her. We were lucky that we had a recent image of her and some sort of resemblance of Tarun for reference. Amelia's facial recognition software had proven to be even more helpful than we originally thought it would be. Even from the grave, my *jaan* was helping us.

CHAPTER IV

AMELIA

A loud noise snapped me awake. Somehow, I had managed to get sleep, maybe even for a few hours. There was no way to tell how long without a clock. I lay on my mattress fully awake but didn't move to avoid attracting any unwanted attention. Maybe, if they thought I was asleep, the guards would leave me alone.

Instead of a lone pair of footsteps echoing in the hall, I heard two. The steps stopped outside of my cell right before the gate creaked. The footsteps sounded again, but this time they moved away from me. Whoever it was must have entered Salena's cell. I slowly angled my head to get a better look at what was happening. There was only one person who dressed as ostentatiously as the figure across the hall.

Decked out in a shimmery orange jacket that reached his knees, Tarun entered her cell as the guard locked it from the outside. I noticed a pile of white cloth in the guard's hands while he waited for his boss.

Tarun's bald head glistened with sweat in the stuffy dungeon. His short stature didn't make him seem threatening at first glance, but there was something in his eyes that drew out my fear. I could see from how Salena cowered in the corner of her cell that she shared my reaction.

"What? No kiss for your soon-to-be husband?" he sneered. Salena looked up at him, frozen to her spot. Tarun knelt in front of her and licked his lips like he was a hyena, and she was a carcass free for the taking.

He stroked a lock of her hair between his fingers. "You need a bath, my love. Any wife of mine must be in pristine condition." *As if she could take a bath without your consent.* She was his doll to dress up and parade around at his whim.

Grabbing her head with his stubby fingers, he shoved his mouth onto hers and took what she didn't want to give. He held her in place for far too long, raping her mouth.

"That's better," he said, letting her go. Her shoulders shook, but still, no sound escaped her.

"Soon enough, you'll take everything I give you on our wedding night," He said moving his hands down her neck and to the curve of her full chest. "You should consider yourself lucky to be engaged to a king like me." He pulled on her breasts like they were squeeze toys, yanking so hard that she flinched from the pain.

I shifted on my mattress anxiously. The coils squeaked under my weight, attracting the attention of the nightmare in jewels across the hall.

"Well, look who's awake!" he said with a flourish. "Perfect, I was just coming to have a meeting with you. Guard, allow me to consult with our computer prodigy." His motions resembled those of a circus ringmaster.

The guard unlocked Salena's gate and granted him entrance to mine. Tarun took the pile of off-white cloth from the guard and approached my mattress, sashaying his hips as he moved. I sat upright, unsure of the safest position to be in. Lying on the floor while he hovered over me probably wasn't the optimal way to face this monster.

"I brought you some new clothes," he said, placing them onto the bench attached to the wall as if he really cared about me. He made a face as he inspected my current outfit. "As beautiful as your current dress is, these would be more *appropriate* for your position here." He eyed my now filthy dress, a rag of its former self. Rips and holes covered the fabric, which was nearly black from being holed up in a dingy cell.

I didn't satisfy him with the thank-you that he sought, yet I was grateful for something clean and hopefully less revealing to wear.

He grabbed my wrists and unlocked the handcuffs around them. My skin there was raw from the metal pressing into it for so long and it stung as the air hit it.

"It's such a shame that your life took this path. It wasn't too long ago that you had a promising future, but then you had to get yourself mixed up with those dreadful Sethi brothers." He clicked his tongue in pity.

"How do you know so much about me?" I asked, willing my voice to stay steady and not show my true fear.

"I have my ways," he said, brushing over my question. "I know that you are quite the computer developer who specializes in facial-recognition software," he continued. "You were able to crack my riddle from the email that I sent your former bosses to figure out that I was here in Jaipur. How you figured out my encryption technique amazes me, especially when that idiot Jai couldn't figure it out on his own."

So, we really are in Jaipur. At least now I knew for sure what city I was in. "Please let me go. I promise I won't tell anyone about you," I begged.

"Not even that dear mother of yours?" His mouth hitched up in a maniacal smile.

I stilled at the mention of my mother. My heart slammed in my chest and panic spread through my body.

"Ah, that's right," he said, grinning at my obvious terror. "I know all about her. The nurse in Seattle, Washington. I think the photo of her next to your bed is most endearing."

How could he know about that photo? I thought back to my time in New York. "You broke into my apartment?" I remembered the time my door was unlocked and I thought I had just been careless, when he actually had one of his goons break in. Was that who was following me at the bar when I called Shyam to pick me up?

He ignored my question, but his smile said everything I needed to know. "What do you think Mummy would say hearing about the trouble her only daughter got herself mixed up with? Her baby girl, aiding and assisting drug dealers? How scandalous! Maybe I should bring her to India so you can explain it to her in person?"

"No, please. I'll do anything, just please don't touch her." I clasped my hands together, praying that he would leave her alone.

He moved his finger to his upper lip, as if considering my plea. "I'm feeling generous today. I do have a position open for you on my team that I think you'd be perfect for."

"What is it?" I asked, knowing it was anything but good.

21

"I want access to all of Shyam and Jai's sales accounts," he said evenly.

"I don't really know how to get all of that for you," I replied nervously. I didn't. I had only ever dealt with tracking and facial-recognition software at Sethi Tech.

His eyes grew furious with rage. He grabbed me by my arms and yanked me close to him. "Don't fuck with me, little girl!" he screamed at me. His face was so close to mine that I could feel his spit fly onto my skin. "I know you have technological permissions to all of their accounts." He slapped me across my face, and I turned with the impact, my cheek stinging. I grasped my face with my hand to ease the pain, my eyes filling with tears.

He took a step backward and straightened his jacket, regaining his composure. "You'll have to excuse me. I am passionate about my work. I'm sure you can see how great of help you could be to me, especially since I have been such a gracious host to you during your stay." His eyes resumed their usual deceitful appearance, not showing any of the rage he had just unleashed on me. He truly was psychotic.

"As far as I see it, you are no longer employed by the Sethi brothers, so you may as well join the winning side. I want access to everything so I can reach out to my new clients that I have acquired and thank them for their patronage. Even your mother would appreciate her daughter working for the right side this time."

He wanted information on all Shyam's distributors so he could sabotage all their pending drug sales. This would completely destroy their business. It was essentially a hostile takeover in the criminal world. And he was using my mother as collateral.

I was too scared to answer him.

He glared at my lack of response. "I can see I've given you a lot to think about it. I'll give you some time to consider my job, offer since I'm such a considerate man."

He moved closer to me and tucked his nose into my neck, sniffing my skin. My stomach churned at his proximity. He brought his mouth to my ear. "Maybe we can get together and sign the contract in private. No need to make wifey over there jealous," he said nodding his head over to Salena's cell. He moved his grubby hands to my abdomen and slid them downward, toward my groin. I felt bile rise up my throat.

He pulled away from me with a grin on his face. "I will be back to hear your acceptance. Guard!" he called, signaling to be let out of the cell, then he turned back before exiting to strike one more arrow into my heart. "Your Mummy would be so proud of you."

He strolled down the hall as the guard locked up the gate and then followed behind, leaving Salena and I alone in our cages in silence, for fear of our captor returning.

23

Chapter V

Amelia

Another period of sunlight shining through the skylight followed by overhead lights in the hallway cycled through. It was never truly dark, so my circadian clock was completely off, making it difficult to sleep during the "night." Although, it was probably safer to stay awake—easier to see danger coming.

Salena had left with a guard a few hours earlier, so I took advantage of the privacy and changed into the clothes Tarun had left for me. It was a long top with matching harem-style pants, like what Salena wore, except it wasn't adorned with embroidery. A matching white shawl was included in the pile. I had seen Salena wear hers around her shoulders and sometimes over her head when she appeared to be deep in thought in her cell.

She was allowed to leave her cell with the guards sometimes. I never asked where she went. She usually came back with a fresh change of clothes on and more bruises on her body. I sensed she was Tarun's punching bag to vent his frustrations on.

Eventually, Salena returned, following a guard. He let her into her cell and left without paying me any attention. *Thank God.* My face still stung from Tarun's slap and my stomach was bruised from being kicked days earlier. I didn't want any more of their attention.

I waited to hear the dungeon door lock before I resumed pacing about my cell. My legs fell asleep often since I was sedentary now, so I wanted to keep my blood circulating by moving about. Though, the walking only slightly distracted me from Tarun's threat on my mom's life.

"How do you know Shyam?" Salena's soft voice interrupted my focus on my steps.

I looked over to find her standing close to the bars of her cell so she wouldn't have to talk loudly for me to hear her. I moved closer to my bars, grabbing them gently. "I work with him."

I decided to spare her the details of our relationship. How could I tell her that I was in love with her ex-fiancé?

Yes. I was *in love* with him. It all seemed so silly, tiptoeing around my feelings for him back in New York. I loved him and might never get the chance to tell him.

"Do you work for his company?" she asked.

"Yes. I'm a software developer." That part was true.

"Oh. How did you know who I was?"

Shit. I hesitated. How could I explain that without giving away more information than needed if I was just his employee? "I saw your picture."

She furrowed her brows. "How?"

"I was helping him locate Tarun before I was kidnapped. Tarun sent Shyam your engagement photo." This was also the truth, but again, not the whole truth. I couldn't tell her that Shyam had first mentioned her while I was on my knees after giving him mind-blowing head. Yeah, that definitely wouldn't make her feel too great.

She looked away in disgust at the mere mention of her engagement. "Shyam saw that? I was wondering what Tarun was doing when he took the photos," she said, her eyes downcast and voice full of shame.

"Yes. Our software was able to decode the coordinates of Jaipur from the photo and catch the reflection of Tarun in the background of your photo," I said.

"Does Shyam know where we are?" she asked hopefully.

I didn't know the answer to that question, so I answered honestly. "I don't know. I hope so."

27

The door down the hall clanked as it shut. Someone was coming. We both hurried back to our benches, putting distance between us so no one would suspect we had been talking.

"You!" the guard shouted at me. "Get up! Boss wants you for work."

Apparently, I no longer had a choice about Tarun's offer. *But then again, does anyone ever have a choice when Tarun is involved?*

The guard opened the cell. I stepped out and followed him, sneaking a glance at Salena on my way out. She looked at me apologetically.

We made our way out of the dungeon and through the door that gave me anxiety every time it made noise, revealing a new *visitor*. The guard pushed me up a long flight of stairs, until I reached the main level of the house, where dingy concrete and chipped paint were replaced by opulent stone and ornate tiles. A large fountain in the middle of the entrance way added a false sense of peacefulness to the ambiance. One wouldn't be able to tell that a raging psycho who kept women prisoners in cages lived in this beautiful palace.

We passed the foyer where I had first met said psycho on the left. The guard shoved me to keep going because I was too busy observing my surroundings instead of walking. I needed to remember the layout of the house if I ever found a chance to escape.

We approached a steel door on my right that didn't fit in with the rest of the extravagant décor of the house. The guard scanned his finger on the biometric scanner at the door, granting us entrance.

The room looked like an old library. Bookcases filled with hardcover books lined the perimeter. Four dark wood tables sat in the center of the room, with two computer stations at each table. A brown chair dotted each station. The musky scent only added to the outdated appearance.

Tarun stood impatiently in the center of the room with his hands on his hips as if he had been waiting for a long time. Today, he was decked out in a purple-and-gold brocade jacket with gold pants. A long necklace strung with pearls adorned his neck, and his mishappened birthmark peeked out from his collar. The gold medallion pendant that sat in the center of the strand of pearls rested on his abdomen. He was as ostentatious as ever.

"Ah, there she is." His voice sounded high-pitched and melodic, like he was singing a song.

"Welcome to your new office, Miss Becker," he exclaimed, waving his hands around. Then he eyed my new outfit.

"I see your *shalwar* fits perfectly."

I looked down at my clothes, unsure how to respond.

"Come, sit down. We have work to accomplish." He motioned at one of the leather chairs.

He pulled the chair out, allowing me to sit. I obeyed his order. His fingers rested on the back of my neck, under my hair, giving me chills on contact. I hated his hands on me. It made me feel violated and dirty.

He inserted a flash drive into the processing unit. *Who uses a flash drive anymore?* The login page for Sethi Tech software was already loaded onto the screen.

"Log in," he commanded me like I was his slave. I obliged without argument. If I protested, I was sure he'd make good on his threat to hurt my mother. She was completely innocent in all of this and I'd die before I'd let him touch her.

I entered my password, then the software prompted me to scan my finger for complete access. I was glad they had never re-cuffed my hands; having them bound would have made working on the keyboard difficult.

I had little experience with the sales accounts. I had only seen Shyam review them a few times, but I had never needed to use them for my work.

After loading the home screen, I accessed the page with all Shyam's clients. Account information for all their distributors were listed, including dates of past shipments, bank account information and contact information, and dates of their next shipments. It was surprising how much drug-dealing sales logs resembled regular online shopping logs. All these dealers needed was an online shopping cart and a website and they'd be set up for home delivery.

A ringing sound echoed through the otherwise silent room, and I breathed a sigh of relief when Tarun removed his hand from my skin to pull out a phone from his pocket. I noticed it was an old-fashioned flip phone. He really was such a strange character. It was like he didn't trust technology, yet he had access to the best of it like Shyam and Jai. Maybe he just didn't want to use a phone with Wi-Fi capability so no one could keep tabs on him. *Paranoid!*

"I'm sorry, Miss Becker. You'll have to excuse me. I have another matter to tend to. I trust you are comfortable enough to continue working in my absence?" His voice was overly considerate, which made me feel even more uneasy.

I nodded silently, hoping that I didn't seem too eager for him to leave.

He barked a warning in what I assumed was Hindi to the guard, then whipped the tail of his jacket around and left the room. "Keep an eye on her and make sure she finishes the job," he shouted in English.

His dual personalities were exhausting to keep up with. It was like he was playing the role of a fabulous host one minute, but he could turn maleficent in a matter of seconds. I never knew what personality I would be dealing with, so I preferred to stay silent to avoid pissing him off. My body couldn't take any more abuse.

The guard looked at me with a menacing look, as if warning me not to try anything funny.

I turned back to the screen and started saving information to the flash drive. Guilt ate at me as I worked. It felt horrible to play a role in destroying Shyam and Jai's business. They would be upset, but what choice did I have? I couldn't let Tarun hurt my mother. They would understand why I did it. Hopefully, they could find a way to fix the damage I was about to cost them.

It took me a while to work through all the accounts. I looked over at the guard, who stood out of view of my monitor. He was intently watching something on his phone out of boredom.

I had a thought. *What if I changed some of the shipping destinations?* All the locations that were receiving shipments soon were either in North America or Europe. None of them were in India. India was Tarun's territory, based on the contract his father had made with Shyam's father. I could send Shyam breadcrumbs about where I was through the sales accounts. I had administrative rights to change anything listed on this page.

The only problem was, I didn't know exactly *where* I was. I knew I was in Jaipur, in a fancy pink palace. Most of the buildings on the drive over here were pink anyways, though, so I guess that wasn't a special detail.

I looked back over to the guard. He was still engrossed in whatever he was doing on his phone. Tarun would be angry if he ever found out how careless his guard was, but *you snooze, you lose.*

They had to have Wi-Fi for the guard to have been watching something on his phone for this long, but I didn't think Tarun would trust Wi-Fi enough, since it would use his location to transmit data about him. Jai would have figured out how to hack it by now.

I opened the web browser. A VPN, or virtual private network, login window popped up. Of course, he was using a VPN for internet! It allowed users to access the internet using encrypted data so that no hackers could see what the person was viewing on the internet. People often used it when they worked from home.

But I was stuck. I had no idea what his password was, and I didn't have much time to figure it out. The guard would surely come over at any moment to hurry me up. I tried random phrases like "Tarun," his brother's name, "Vik," and even Shyam and Jai's names. No luck.

I knew it was a long shot to guess the password correctly. It could be anything. The possibilities were endless, and I had limited time.

My eyes strayed to a painting on the wall. *A Bengal Tiger.* Tarun's family crest. These crests were important to Shyam and Tarun's family histories.

I typed in "Tiger" out of curiosity. *Access denied.* Hastily, I tried "Bengal Tiger." *It worked!* It was a bit surprising that his password was so simple and without any special characters or numbers, but regardless, I had access to the internet and maps.

I quickly researched names of businesses in Jaipur. I still couldn't figure out my current location since Tarun had blocked GPS on his network to keep it secure. However, I was able to find names of businesses that made sweets, shoes, and anything else that I could use an address from to change the existing addresses for shipments on the accounts. These places would possibly be getting hefty, surprise packages of drugs, but I hoped Shyam would notice something was off before that ever happened. I was desperate.

I noticed the name of a Jaipur company that produced fabrics. It was called Mongoose Inc.

I recalled the conversation I had with Shyam when I first asked about the cobra on his ring. He had said that the one animal that could kill the deadly cobra was the mongoose.

34

Now I was hoping he would remember that conversation too. I guessed I would soon find out.

I pulled the flash drive from the computer. I had done what Tarun asked of me, and he wouldn't know that I had changed the addresses if I never saved my changes to the flash drive.

I changed the addresses to the random local business addresses that I had found, including Mongoose Inc. I used that address about six times for various shipments while only using the other unique addresses I found once, hoping Mongoose Inc. would stand out to Shyam.

The guard approached the computer. I quickly saved my changes onto the software portal and logged out, also closing the maps I had been using. I logged out of the VPN server too.

"Done!" I exclaimed, relieved to have cleared up any evidence in time. I handed the flash drive over to the guard, who pocketed it before leading me outside.

I prayed this would work and that *this* time, the cobra came to seek out the mongoose.

CHAPTER VI

SHYAM

J ai burst into my office, holding his laptop. "You have to see this."

"Don't you ever knock?" I asked, annoyed, and looked up from the reports I was reviewing. Although my main priorities were getting Amelia's body back and seeking vengeance, I couldn't neglect my duties at Sethi Tech any longer.

Ignoring me, he walked over to my side of the desk and plopped his computer right on top of my papers without any regard for my work.

I sat back in my chair and let out an exasperated sigh. When Jai was this focused on something it was impossible to get him to snap out of it. I blamed it on the computer engineer in him—insanely focused.

I didn't have the energy to kick him out of my office because work was taking every ounce I had left in me. I still couldn't get much sleep without waking up from nightmares of Amelia being taken.

I stared the monitor. "Why am I looking at our sales accounts?" I asked. Our business had slowed down considerably, so the listings were thinner than usual.

"Look at the shipping addresses," he said, jabbing a finger at the screen in frustration.

I examined each of our upcoming scheduled shipments. Listings where product should be shipped to locations like Greece or the Dominican Republic all had shipping addresses in Jaipur. This could only mean that Tarun had successfully infiltrated our sales software. Up until now, he had sabotaged our business mostly by destroying our shipments or intercepting them before they were delivered. But now, he was redirecting entire shipments before they even left our docks.

I furrowed my brow, trying to figure out the point of such a move. "Why would he want all of that product in Jaipur?"

"I have no clue. I get that he might want us to see that he has full control over our accounts now, but I don't know what he plans to do with all our product. He has his own to distribute, and a lot of it."

"All the addresses are for different locations in Jaipur, too," I mentioned.

"Why go through all that trouble collecting product at different sites? That just seems like extra work for him."

I looked closer at the addresses to see if I recognized any of them. They seemed to belong to various businesses in the city but none of them looked familiar. The companies were all unique, except for Mongoose Inc. It was listed several times, which I found odd.

I took over Jai's laptop and looked up the company. It belonged to a small fabric factory.

Jai studied what I was doing. "Why is Mongoose Inc. listed so frequently?"

I sat back in my chair, deep in thought. Why would he choose Mongoose Inc. in particular?

My thoughts played like a video. I remembered a children's book my mother used to read to me about a mongoose. I recalled a conversation I had with Amelia before she was kidnapped. She had asked if any animal could defeat the cobra, which was on my family crest. I had told her about the mongoose. I had even called her "my little mongoose," because she would be the death of me.

And here, a company called Mongoose Inc. was listed more than once in a string of unique addresses. It could all just be a random coincidence. There were lots of companies in India with "Mongoose" in the name. Yet, why this one in particular, and in Jaipur of all places—the city where Tarun's last photo was taken?

My heart was racing. I knew in my gut what this meant.

I pushed my chair back and stood up. I had to start preparing. "Tell Saran to get the plane ready. We're leaving for India, now."

"Why?" Jai asked, utterly confused, as he shut his laptop.

"Amelia is alive."

CHAPTER VII

AMELIA

"You! Fucking cunt!"

I sat up on my mattress, startled by Tarun's aggressive screams. Salena yelped in her cell like a frightened puppy.

The guard accompanying him opened my cell, allowing Tarun to bolt toward me so fast that I couldn't get away in time. His hands were on my neck, pinning me to the mattress. He squeezed hard, closing off my trachea. I clawed at his hands in a desperate attempt to loosen his grip. I kicked my bare feet frantically, hoping to get him off me. I couldn't breathe.

"You didn't think I'd find out? After everything I've done for you as your host. And *this* is how you repay me?" His hold on me tightened and black spots began to dance in front of my eyes. "You changed all of the shipping addresses, sneaky bitch."

I felt my consciousness slipping as my eyelids drooped.

He loosened his hands on my throat but straddled me to keep me from getting away. Immediately, I gasped for air. My throat burned as air rushed into my lungs, causing me to fall into a fit of coughing.

He pulled out a knife from his pocket and pressed the point into the flesh of my cheek. I felt a sharp pinch as the blade pierced my skin. Tears streamed down to my hair as I looked at the maniac on top of me. I was scared to talk, for fear of him sinking his knife even further into my face.

"When I give an order, I expect my employees to listen." His crazed eyes were full of malice. He sliced the knife along my cheek and searing pain heated the side of my face when I felt the warm trickle of blood slide down to my ear. I screamed in agony.

He withdrew the blade, waving it in the air as he spoke. "You will pay for defying my orders." He moved closer to carve my flesh again.

"Wait!" I begged. "I was just trying to help. Please believe me."

He cocked his head to one side, studying my face with curiosity. His mannerisms were steady which made him more terrifying. "Explain."

I didn't know how he found out what I did, but I needed to talk fast to convince him that I was only trying to help him destroy Shyam to save my skin, literally. "I thought that if I replaced all the addresses for their upcoming orders, it would help to sabotage their business."

He sat back, allowing me to slide out from under him and sit up right. Blood dripped down from my cut to my neck.

"You think I am a fool? Why would you want to help me when your alliances clearly lie elsewhere?" He was rightfully skeptical.

"I wanted to do anything to keep my mom safe," I pled.

"I can respect that. Family is important in our culture," he said calmly.

"She means everything to me," I said through my tears, my lower lip quivering from emotion. It was easy to persuade him of my motives since my love for my mom was true.

He seemed to have bought my explanation because he stood and adjusted his coat to smooth out the wrinkles. He pulled out a handkerchief from his pocket and threw it at me.

"A gentleman always carries a handkerchief in case a lady should ever find herself in need of one. Clean yourself up," he said, posing as the picture of decorum. *Some gentleman.*

Before exiting the cell, he turned back toward me. "Your actions *do* work in my favor, but I'm keeping my eye on you.

Consider *that* your final warning," he said pointing to my cheek. Then he left the dungeon with his guard.

I pressed the handkerchief to my wound, careful not to press too hard. It stung on contact. I pulled the cloth away to examine the damage. He must have cut deep because it was soaked in blood.

I looked over to Salena, whose eyes were full of concern. She did her best to offer me silent comfort.

"Please find us, Shyam," I whispered through clenched teeth in prayer.

CHAPTER VIII

SHYAM

The engines roared to life, vibrating the entire vessel. Marie, my private flight attendant, made her way around the cabin to ensure that our seatbelts were securely fastened. The pilot came onto the intercom to let us know that we would be ready to take off shortly. Jai and our men were busy discussing details of the plan I had drafted for them.

All of it sounded like background noise to me. I could only focus on one thought. *Amelia is alive.*

I sat in my seat next to the window with my aviators on—a sign that I did not want to be disturbed by anyone. Even Marie took the hint and silently glanced at my lap, inspecting my fastened seatbelt without uttering a word to me.

How did I not realize she was alive? I had been beating myself up over that question since I found the clues she left on our sales software. So many days had passed while I moped over her death like a waste of space when she was actually alive, and at the mercy of my nemesis. I had seen evidence of his treatment from the bruises on Salena in her engagement photo... my imagination was running wild with how he must be treating my woman.

It was no secret that Jai and I weren't easy when administering punishments to those who had wronged us, but we didn't necessarily *enjoy* it. Tarun did. He was a known maniac that got off on twisted shit—not just fucking with a person physically, but mentally, too. He was sick in the head, and so were his men. They were vile creatures that found enjoyment in torturing women and even children. I had never needed to punish a woman, let alone a child, in all my years of doing business.

Visions of Amelia with bruises covering her naked body played in my head like a horror movie. What if they had forced themselves on her? I gripped the arm rests, ready to pull them off their screws. Nothing would get in the way of my wrath. I would kill them all with my bare hands for taking her away from me.

Amelia was smart, though. I didn't know how she had managed to pull this off. Without a doubt, Tarun had her under close watch, wherever she was. He knew she was a computer genius and that was why he took her. He also knew that she was a significant person in my life, which made her more valuable in his eyes. I was almost certain he had used her to hack into our records, but how she'd managed to change shipping addresses to Mongoose Inc. impressed me. We had only discussed the meaning of the mongoose once. She was brilliant for choosing such a subtle clue, and Tarun was oblivious to its meaning. If he ever found out what she did, Amelia's life would be at risk.

A lump settled in my throat when I thought of losing her again. I took a sip of my scotch, allowing the smooth liquid to soothe my worries. I had always been a big scotch drinker, but in recent days, it had gone beyond "social drinking" to "necessity." It kept me sane by numbing my insides.

But now that Amelia was waiting for me in India, I needed to remain lucid. I couldn't save her if I were drunk, so I put my drink down.

Eighteen hours later, we landed in Amritsar, in the north of my home state of Punjab. I hadn't been home in about two years. Jai and I rarely returned since our mother was killed by Tarun and our dad subsequently killed himself out of grief. We never needed to go back unless it was related to business.

I paused at the top of the stairs as I exited the plane, inhaling the humid air. December usually brought cooler temperatures, but the stagnant air of the city made it feel hotter. To most people, the thick smog that blanketed Punjab was stifling. To me, it just smelled like home.

I buttoned my suit jacket before descending the stairs onto the tarmac. Blacked-out vehicles were already waiting to transport us to my family home.

A tall figure towered in front of the fleet of cars. "*Bhaiya.*" *Brother.* Zayn greeted me with a warm smile. We had basically been raised as brothers, even though we weren't blood. "It's good to see you. Welcome home." He patted me on the back.

"Thank you, brother," I replied. It was good to see him, too. He had a warm quality he showed to those closest to him that countered his threatening physique. He was the tallest of our men and probably the most lethal. He was heavily trained in mixed martial arts and had even left for Thailand to train as a Muay Thai fighter a few years back. He prided himself on always being honest and fair and had been the voice of reason whenever Jai and I argued when we were younger.

We boarded the cars and started our journey home. Zayn knew that I wanted to get straight to work and didn't stall for another moment.

"We have men staking out all locations listed on the sales log, with heavier surveillance on Mongoose Inc. like you asked. We know that Tarun's men are monitoring each location, too, and have set up camera systems outside of each business to monitor activity." He stilled for a moment, as if considering his next words carefully. "How sure are you that this woman is alive?"

I hadn't told him the details of my relationship with Amelia, but he knew me too well to not realize she was a person of significance in my life since I was doing everything in my power to find her.

"I just know," I said bluntly.

He pressed further, despite knowing that I wasn't in the mood to be argued with. "Have you considered that this might just be a trap? Tarun is itching to get his hands on you."

I had thought of that, but he couldn't have known about my discussion about the mongoose with her. It was too random of a conversation, which was how I knew Amelia was using it to send me a message that she was still alive. "The sales log wasn't hacked. Someone who had administrative rights accessed it. Tarun wouldn't have been able to access it without hacking unless he had someone from our team to do it for him."

My explanation seemed to be sufficient for Zayn. "Fair enough. However, I don't think we should act rashly. He has eyes on each location and someone that we want back…alive."

I rubbed the scruff on my jaw. I didn't reply, even though he was right. Instead, I just turned my body to stare out the window.

We had made our way out of the crowded city and into the countryside. The air was clearer here, allowing the blue sky peek out from behind pillowy white clouds. Lush green grass lined either side of the village road. In the distance, I could see farmers tilling their land with bulls with sharp horns. The familiar sound of cowbells chimed through the windows of the car.

We passed through the steel gates, stopping in front of our palace. Since we were in the village, the ornate building spanned acres of land that would never have been possible had it been in the city. Here, I never had to worry about looters invading the house. The villagers were trustworthy and were not ones to rob their neighbors.

I hadn't been back for some time, but the house continued to run in my absence with the help of caretakers and staff to maintain its pristine condition. However, since hearing about our visit, the staff had doubled in size, judging from the line of people waiting to greet us out front. The head of staff, Raj, stood with his hands folded over his large waist. He had been my father's butler and had taken care of Jai and I as his own children over the years.

I stepped out of the car and Raj approached me, bowing as was customary for staff to do to their bosses out of respect, even though Raj was decades older than me. I stopped him before he touched his hand to my shoe. "You don't need to do that, Raj." I had never been a fan of this tradition, though it was the custom, and especially not with Raj, since he was a father figure to me.

"Welcome home, *saab.*" *Sir.* Raj was a man of etiquette and decorum, so I knew he would never stop bowing to me, even when he reached his eighties. He grabbed my hands in his and squeezed them, showing his gratitude for my return. Jai joined my side and Raj performed the whole ritual of bowing again, though Jai stopped him from doing so too. "Please, come inside. I will have your bags carried to your rooms and dinner will be ready in one hour."

I roamed the spacious hallways, decorated with art pieces depicting various scenes of Indian life. My mother had always loved that we lived in the village with lots of greenery and open skies, so she had decorated the walls with pieces reflecting the lifestyle. Paintings of women preparing butter in old-fashioned churning apparatuses and men using machetes to cut down trees adorned the halls.

I wandered into what used to be my father's office before I took over the business. Dark mahogany trims framed the space. The smell of dust and leather from years of being abandoned assaulted my nostrils as I stood in the doorway. The curtains were drawn, limiting any natural light into the room. I flicked on the switch for the light before venturing inside.

51

I sat behind the wood desk, the leather chair creaking under my weight. I smoothed my hands over the tabletop. Years later, and it was still difficult to adjust to the idea that my parents were gone. It was easier to ignore it all in New York, where city life and Sethi Tech served as a distraction. But here in the countryside, in my parents' home, I couldn't hide from the memories of being raised by two loving parents.

I understood how my father had felt when Tarun brutally raped and murdered my mother. His heart had died. I had felt it when I thought Amelia was dead. I wasn't sure how much longer I could have lived knowing that she had left this Earth.

But now I *knew* she was alive. I swore to myself that I wouldn't let history repeat itself and I would bring her home and always keep her safe.

CHAPTER IX

AMELIA

"Do you think Shyam will figure it out?" Salena whispered across her cell. After Tarun discovered the altered shipping addresses and subsequently slit my cheek open, needless to say, Selena had a few questions for me. She had heard most of the story, but I filled in the most pertinent details.

"I hope so," I whispered back carefully, making sure no one could hear me. My incision stung whenever I moved my mouth to speak. "Do you know exactly where we are right now? I tried to access our location through the Wi-Fi, but I wasn't able to, and I'm not sure the VPN was accurate."

"When I was younger, I used to travel to Jaipur often with my father. I believe we're somewhere on Chandni Road."

I had seen that location on the map when I was looking up addresses to add to the sales log. "This house is huge. How do people not suspect that Tarun lives here?"

"The rest of the city thinks an old man lives in this house. No one can get in or out of the gates without him knowing, so people can't really get a good look inside. Tarun had a rumor spread that a reclusive widower lives here and wants privacy. They made it sound like the person was eccentric, and the public never bothered to figure out more information since they believed it was an elderly person."

"How do you know all of this?" I was astonished because I was fairly sure that Tarun hadn't openly told her everything.

"They trust me because I don't put up a fight. I overheard the guards talking one day when they were carrying me upstairs. They figured that I had nobody to talk to, and since my father basically handed me over to Tarun, I wouldn't be able to run away or rat them out anyway. My father would make sure of it," she replied, sulking in disappointment.

It had to have been hard knowing that your own father thought of you as his property to give to another man. "I'm sorry about that, Salena. You don't deserve this life."

Her eyes watered as she stared at me. "Thank you. I wish I were as smart as you to try to escape. I never tried because I thought it would be pointless. I would have nowhere to run to. They would find me wherever I went."

"You're smarter than you realize. The fact that you've stayed alive this long without them killing you proves it." I looked into her eyes before making my vow. "We'll make it out of here... together. I promise you."

A wide smile spread across her face, reaching her eyes. She really was a beautiful woman with soft, delicate features. I had once been jealous of her and everything that she once had, but now she was my friend.

"There's a small fabric shop called Mongoose Inc. that I used as an address to tip off Shyam," I continued. "Do you know where that is? I think I saw that it's on Mount Road."

"Hmmm..." She furrowed her brows, considering my question. "I think I know it. It's a small, rundown building near one of the big temples. I used to go to that temple whenever we were in town and I remember seeing the sign for Mongoose Inc. on our way there. I can't believe it's still in business."

"I need to get there. Shyam and Jai are probably monitoring each of the locations that I used to divert their shipments. I'm hoping that if I get to that location, they'll see me and can help us." I hoped that they would think to take pictures of anyone passing by the locations, especially Mongoose Inc., so that it would trigger the facial-recognition software. Shyam would know I had been there if my photo found a match against the software. I hadn't figured out every detail of my plan yet, but it was a start.

Before Salena could answer, the dungeon door opened. Instinctually, Salena and I backed further into our respective cells just before Tarun waltzed down the hall, stopping between them.

"Great news!" he exclaimed, clasping his hands over his chest. His iridescent blue jacket shimmered under the skylight. "Your plan worked, Ms. Becker. My sales have increased tenfold since you worked your magic on Shyam's sales accounts. I have been busy welcoming my new clients all day. I'm even thinking of preparing a party to properly thank them for their business." He clapped his hands in excitement, looking expectantly at me to reciprocate his glee.

"That's…umm…wonderful," I said, but it came out more confused than happy.

"I have to say, I was suspicious of your motives, little girl, but you proved your worth to me. I think I might just keep you on board as Vice President of Sales." His words were flying out so fast and his hands flailing so enthusiastically that I felt dizzy.

He continued without waiting for my reaction, his hands now on his hips. "Your boyfriend is suspicious, though. He has his men watching all the locations that you entered, probably to steal back the merchandise that was rerouted. Of course, he is no match for my army." His face shone with his perceived victory. "It surprises me as to why you were bedding him in the first place when you are much smarter than him. Seems like such a waste of time." He shook his head in mock disappointment and changed the topic. "Anyway, one wrong move and his men are dead." He grinned with psychotic satisfaction.

It had worked! Shyam knew something was off. Now I just needed for his men to get a photo of me at one of those locations to trigger the software. Maybe I could hide out at Mongoose Inc. long enough for one of his men to rescue me. I needed to find a way to get out of this cell.

I chanced a glance at Salena. I hadn't told her exactly how I knew Shyam; all I had said was that I worked with him because I thought it would have been a little awkward to tell her I had screwed her ex-fiancé. Now, I wished I had told her the truth.

Her lips were pursed and expression twisted in bitterness. *Dammit.* I'd betrayed her. I felt awful for having kept information from her, especially when she had been so honest with me. I genuinely liked her and hated that she'd had to find out this way.

"I just thought of the most wonderful idea for a party," Tarun's voice pierced through my thoughts. "Get ready, wife," he exclaimed, moving closer to Salena's cell, "we're getting married in four days!"

With a flourish of his jacket, he turned and spun away, walking hastily down the hall. The door slammed, leaving Salena and I alone in awkward silence.

CHAPTER X

SHYAM

"We can't ambush each of the locations blindly. We aren't even certain that she's in Jaipur," Jai said, leaning against a bookcase in my father's office.

"Of course, they are," I said. "All of the addresses listed were ones in Jaipur."

"How do we know that Tarun isn't on the run again? He would have taken her with him too," Saran asked, seated in a chair across from my desk. His mammoth arms poked out over the sides of the chair; it was too small to contain him.

"We can't be completely sure of where he is, but we do know that Jaipur was of some significance for her to use addresses within that city. Therefore, we still need heavy surveillance at all locations mentioned. It's possible that we can find clues in Jaipur that he *is* on the move," Zayn chimed in sensing my growing frustration at everyone doubting my intuition. I knew Amelia was in Jaipur, but it was a feeling that only I could sense. I couldn't blame my brother and my men for being skeptical.

"I guess that makes sense, since we don't have much to go off of," Jai said, rubbing his chin as he considered Zayn's argument. "We'll need to make sure that photos are being taken of all people passing by the locations. I can allow our surveillance men to have access to the software. All the photos they take will be automatically scanned and uploaded to the cloud. We should get a hit if Amelia, Tarun, or even Salena are photographed, since we already have their images saved."

"Make sure you and I both get notifications on our phones if we do get a hit," I reminded him. I wanted to know as soon as any of them were found.

He nodded in understanding.

We spent the next three hours combing through each location using virtual maps to memorize exactly how they looked from overhead and street views. We also allocated more men for surveillance.

After we adjourned for the day, the guys headed to the dining room for some of Raj's famous *biriyani*, made with seasoned rice and lamb marinated in yogurt. The men wanted to fill their bellies before we departed for Jaipur tonight.

I wasn't hungry so I opted to walk the gardens out back. Even though our palace was spacious inside, the anxiety I was experiencing from the search left me feeling claustrophobic. I needed some fresh air.

The house wrapped around a courtyard with six large fountains and a massive swimming pool in the middle. A lush green garden sat off to the end of the courtyard and extended past the confines of the house. The musical chirping of birds soothed my mind. Mango and lychee trees spanned the landscape. Jasmine vines sprawled along trellises in the shape of arches. The air was fragrant with perfume and nectar.

The winds had begun to pick up and clouds settled overhead. A storm was coming.

I used to run around these grounds eating fruit from the trees with my brother and Zayn when we were children. We'd pretend to launch rocket ships using soda bottles and balloons. It would make a huge mess, but Raj would cover for us and hide all evidence of our mischief from my father. We'd play until the sun disappeared and the crickets chirped in the evening air. My mother would have to come herd us indoors to eat dinner and take baths. Even though she had servants to do all of that for her, she was still a hands-on mother who took care of us. Her parenting style reflected her upbringing. She was born in this same village, in a meager household of farmers, and never lost the desire to do things for herself. Now that I was an adult, I could appreciate that quality in her.

I saw the same traits in Amelia. She was a hard worker who was unafraid of struggle. She was unfazed by my wealth and power. Most women threw themselves at me because of the things I could buy them. However, she was reluctant to accept any of the perks that Sethi Tech or I gave her. She even seemed awkward at the office because it was so lavish. I admired her humility.

Soon, we would travel to Jaipur undercover and set up headquarters there while we searched for Amelia. I had a family acquaintance who owned a hotel and was willing to check us in under pseudonyms to avoid suspicion. We would leave at nightfall so as not to risk being seen in broad day light. I wanted to be in the city if she were found so I could get to her as quickly as possible.

A cool breeze blew in, carrying droplets of rain with it. They splashed on my face, dripping down my neck and wetting my shirt. I should have turned back to the house to dry up, but I stayed. I let the rain wash over me. Water was used for cleansing in our culture, to prepare one to receive blessings. I wasn't particularly religious, but this rain felt like a preparation for my blessing from the gods—getting my love back.

Chapter XI

Amelia

S alena hadn't spoken to me since Tarun left. She was upset and I could feel the tension radiating off her from
my cell. I felt bad that she'd had to find out about my
relationship with Shyam so suddenly. She probably already had
major trust issues from being held captive and I had ruined any
sort of trust we had built by not being upfront.

I threaded my arms through the bars of my cell, grabbing
the cold metal with my hands. Pressing my face closely, I spoke
in a low voice. "I'm sorry I didn't tell you."

"Tell me what? That you were fucking my ex?" Angry eyes
flashed in my direction. She looked like she would have stran-
gled me if there hadn't been bars between us.

"It's not like that. I wanted to tell you, but I knew it would be awkward and I couldn't find the right words to explain it."

"I'm not angry that you're his girlfriend. I didn't expect him to stay celibate after we ended things, but I'm hurt that you weren't honest with me."

"I know. I'm really sorry." I dropped my head in shame. "For what it's worth, I'm not his girlfriend."

She looked at me, her forehead creased from confusion. "But I heard Tarun. You were sleeping with him, yes?" She seemed genuinely confused.

"Um—yeah. But we weren't officially together."

"Because of his commitment issues?" she asked, as if all of this was familiar to her.

"He said he wouldn't settle down because he respected marriage too much to bring a wife into all of this," I said, waving my arms around.

"He took the death of his mother pretty hard and even broke off our engagement after his father passed."

"Please, Salena. Don't let this get in the way of us getting out of here," I pled. "I need your help. You know this city better than me." I needed her help if I had any chance of breaking out of here.

She considered my plea for a moment, then yelled, "Guard!"

This was it. She was going to take her revenge on me for sleeping with her ex-fiancé and rat me out. Tarun would surely kill me for attempting to escape.

A guard approached her cell, glaring at her for disturbing him. I held my breath before Salena continued.

"I would like to go to the temple tomorrow to pray for my mother before my wedding. Please ask Tarun for permission." Her voice was the steadiest I had ever heard it. Like she really was the soon-to-be wife of a kingpin. Something told me this was more like the real Salena, the one that had been engaged to Shyam. Confident and authoritative.

The guard grunted in acknowledgment and stomped away.

I stared at Salena, uncertain of what had just transpired. None of it made sense.

She walked to the bench in her cell. Sliding her hand under it, she pulled out a long, thick rope that had been hidden away.

She marched back to the bars of her cell and threw it to me. I caught it through the bars and held it close to my face to examine it.

Her face was unreadable. "Don't screw this up."

***

Fortunately, Tarun had granted Salena permission to go to the temple. Apparently, she had been allowed to go once before her engagement ceremony too. Her mother had died years ago, and it was customary to honor deceased relatives before participating in life events like marriages.

"Will your father be attending the wedding?" I asked. I knew her father was an evil man who would sell his daughter in exchange for a penny if it would benefit him.

"I'm sure he'll be there. He's supposed to give me away, according to tradition." She still seemed hostile toward me for keeping the truth of my relationship with Shyam from her but at least she was speaking to me again.

"Does he know how you've been treated here?"

"Yes. He's just as evil as Tarun so I'm sure he doesn't care." Salena's sagged. It couldn't have been easy knowing your father didn't mind you were being kept as someone's personal punching bag.

I decided to change the topic. We had more important matters at hand than discussing her poor excuse of a father. "So, you said a handmaid went with you last time you visited the temple?"

"Yes, men aren't allowed in the area of the temple that I prayed in, so Tarun made Noor escort me in case I tried to run away. She's the maid who helps me dress."

"You mean when the guards take you out of your cell?" I had always wondered where she went when they took her away for hours almost every day.

"Most of the time it's for daily grooming, but other times I have to visit Tarun." Her tone implied that there was more to the visit than small talk. My heart broke for her. I was lucky to have avoided being raped while here. I thought Tarun had spared me from that type of hell because I was useful to him in other ways, but Salena hadn't been so lucky.

"I promise you we're going to get out of here." My voice strong with confidence. I had to believe it to protect my sanity. "You said that Noor wears a burkah?"

"Yes, she's a very conservative Muslim. Tarun mostly has Hindu and Sikh women working for him, but lucky for us, she is one of the few Muslims here and wears all black fabric that covers her face. You can disguise yourself with her clothes and no one will suspect it's you unless they check your cell."

I wasn't sure how I'd go about getting Noor's clothes. I knew that she'd be waiting for Salena in front of the garage in a few hours before they left for the temple in the car. Salena helped me fill in the gaps I had in my mental map of the house. I just needed to figure out how to get out of my cell and get to Noor without anyone else seeing me. I stowed the rope away under the bench in my cell just as Salena had so no one could see it if they just glanced around.

After reaching the temple, I would need to get to Mount Road and find Mongoose Inc. I prayed that the directions that

Salena remembered were correct. My hope was that one of Shyam's men would have eyes on the factory and take photos of me. If all went as planned, the photo would trigger the facial-recognition system as soon as it was uploaded to the cloud.

That was another issue. Hopefully, all surveillance photos would be set to upload to the cloud automatically; otherwise, the software wouldn't work.

My plan after that was to hide out nearby. My red hair and light skin made me stand out in India. I'd have to stay in my disguise so Tarun's men wouldn't find me.

I worried about what Tarun would do to Salena when he found out I had escaped. I couldn't take her with me because she had a tracker in her ankle. Tarun had injected one into her before her first outing to the temple. We had planned for her to stay at the temple alone, so no one suspected anything was off. Hopefully, they'd believe that she had nothing to do with me escaping. We agreed that I would come back to get her from the mansion once I had Shyam's men as reinforcements. It wasn't a solid plan at all, but we had to make it work somehow. We wouldn't get another opportunity like this.

As we expected, a guard came to escort Salena away. She would be taken away for about an hour before leaving the palace to be groomed and dressed for the temple. I waited several minutes to make sure Salena was upstairs and hopefully being attended by Noor as she dressed.

I grabbed the rope from the underside of the bench, and I wrapped it on itself a few times to ensure it would be strong enough to handle what I was about to use it for. Tucking it into the waistband of my pants, I adjusted my top over it fully cover any evidence of what I was hiding. I was glad that this style of outfit included a loose-fitting top. It was easy to disguise something under it.

I approached the bars of my cage, willing my hands to stop shaking from nerves. I took a deep and steadying breath to calm myself down.

Smoothing my hand over my cheek, I felt the thick scab that had formed where Tarun had sliced my cheek open. I felt the bumpy ridges of the tough sheathing.

My nails hadn't been groomed since I had been taken, so they were a lot longer than usual. I dug them under the scab and ripped it off. It crumbled off in pieces, so I had to try multiple times to remove all of it. Tears sprang to my eyes and I squeezed them shut against the pain. At last, my cheek felt wet, signifying success. I rubbed my fingers over it and examined the liquid. Blood, but not nearly as much as I had hoped for. Taking another deep breath, I used my nails to scratch the cut open even further, digging deep inside. I was sure it would become infected from shoving my dirty nails into it, but it was a small price to pay.

My stomach turned from the sensation, and I was already queasy from the pain. I would throw up if I thought too hard about what I was doing, so I just focused on my breathing. *Inhale. Exhale.* Warm liquid oozed down my face, dripping onto my clothes. That was surely enough for what I needed.

I grabbed the bars and shook them, "Guard! Guard!"

A short, stocky man hurried to the cell. Panic set into his eyes as he saw blood splashed all over me.

"Please! Help me!" I begged, letting the tears spill from my eyes. I needed to convince him that I was truly freaked out.

He opened the gate and rushed inside, leaving the gate open.

"What is the meaning of this?" he shouted, not knowing what to do.

I sobbed loudly. "My wounded opened up again! I don't know how!" My reaction was mostly genuine because I was in excruciating pain. The guard looked around for anything to use as an aid, his head bobbing around like a caged chicken.

"The handkerchief," I shouted as I clutched my cheek. I pointed to the bloodied one that Tarun had given to me days ago, neatly folded on the bench behind me.

He eyed me with suspicion, not moving for fear it was a trick. "Please!" I screamed.

That got him to fulfill my request. He turned his back to me and rushed to the far end of my cell to retrieve the cloth.

I slipped my hand under the back of my top and into the waistband of my pants, feeling for the rope. My heart was pounding through my chest, but I forced myself to move quickly behind the guard as he bent over to pick up the fabric. My bare feet fell silently on the concrete. Before he could stand up straight, I slid the folded rope over his head and pulled it as tight as I could around his neck. He made choking sounds as he tried to pull it off his neck. His knees gave out bringing both of us to the ground. The ends of the rope started slipping out of my sweaty grasp as he fought against me. I pulled harder, with everything I had, my biceps burning from the struggle. Sick gurgling filled the cell as his body crouched to the floor. I thrashed along with his every move, never letting up on the noose. Suddenly, his hands went limp and he toppled to the ground, his body no longer moving. His eyes were wide, staring up at the ceiling.

Fuck. I was in shock over having had just killed someone. This was the plan all along but now that it had happened, I felt myself start to shake uncontrollably. *Breathe, Becker.* I reminded myself to focus and that it was not the time to give into panic.

I eyed the gun in his holster. I had never used one myself, but I knew that you had to remove the safety before pulling the trigger from seeing my dad use them when I lived at home. I looped the rope I had just used on the guard around my neck like a necklace since I would probably need to use it again soon.

71

I grabbed the gun and tucked into my waistband. It couldn't hurt to have one just in case I needed it later—since now I was a cold-blooded killer and all. Bile rose up my throat. *Focus, Becker.*

Salena would be nearly finished dressing, so I had to hurry. I retrieved the dropped handkerchief that had slipped from the guard's hand onto the ground and pressed it against my cheek to sop up some of the blood so I wouldn't leave a drip trail behind me. My cheek stung on contact, I had to press my lips together to stop from screaming aloud. I grabbed the keyring from the waist of the guard's pants, too.

I slid out of the opened gate quietly and made my way to the dungeon door. No one was in the hallway. I tried each of the three keys on the ring when I reached the door, and the last one opened it. I knew this door was the noisiest one, so I pushed it open as gently as possible to minimize the sound it made.

My heartbeat was pounding in my ears as I made my way into the palace. I looked around the corner and no one was in sight. I followed along the walls of the perimeter, as Salena had instructed. I could hear distant chatter from females—probably the maids. Instead of coming toward me, they took a turn and their voices moved further away.

I crossed the hallway by the kitchen, slipping past the cooking staff.

At the end of the hall, I spotted Noor. She was cloaked in all black, standing next to a freshly dressed Salena in front of the door to the garage. Salena's head was covered in a headscarf. They were waiting for a guard to open the door so they could get into one of the cars.

I ducked into the shadows to avoid being noticed by Noor. I held my breath as I tiptoed along the wall. Salena noticed me but didn't make it obvious so as not to draw Noor's attention.

I approached them, staying in the shadows of the statues and sculptures that decorated the hall. Just as Noor noticed me, Salena reached out in a flash and slapped her palm against her mouth through her *burkah* to muffle her. I ran towards them and helped Salena wrestle her down to the ground.

We had to move quickly, before the guard opened the door. I grabbed the rope from my neck and moved to tie Noor's hands behind her back.

"No, take her clothes first," Salena whispered, struggling to hold her hand over Noor's mouth to keep her quiet. For an older woman, the handmaid knew how to put up a fight.

I couldn't figure out how to undress her. Her robes were so long, and there wasn't a zipper or any buttons that I could see.

Other than her hands, Noor's eyes were the only part of her body that was exposed, and they were wild with fear.

Salena noticed my struggle. "Did you steal a gun?"

I nodded and removed it from my waist band. Salena grabbed it from me, removed the safety, and aimed it at Noor. "*Uth jao,*" Salena whispered forcefully.

As if following her command, Noor stood up silently, despite her mouth no longer being covered. Salena pushed the gun into the small of Noor's back and pushed her to the side of the hall, in front of a door. Opening it, she shoved Noor inside and left the door open for me to follow. It seemed like we were inside of a supply closet.

"Hand me that drop cloth," she ordered, nodding her head to a pile of fabric neatly folded on the ground by the door. She pulled off Noor's head covering, revealing an elderly woman with wiry silver hair pulled into an unkempt bun. Her face was full of wrinkles and she had a few missing teeth. She didn't look like the most agreeable woman—more cranky and perhaps even mean. The woman started to whine in a foreign tongue. Salena pushed the gun further into her face. "*Chup!*" That instantly shut her up.

I handed the rolled-up drop cloth to Salena, unsure of what she would need it for. As if she had done this many times before, she pressed the cloth to the old woman's temple and touched end of the gun to the cloth. In one quick move, she pulled the trigger. With barely a sound, Noor slumped onto the floor, lifeless.

I stood frozen to my spot, staring at the dead woman in front me. Salena saw how stunned I was. "What? She was a horrible bitch. She deserved it for how she treated me."

"How—how did you do that—like—"

"You forget that I'm the daughter of a criminal and have been engaged to two of them, as well." A sly smile spread across her lips, as if she were proud her background. She was more badass than I had given her credit for.

"Stop standing there and come get dressed," she ordered.

Salena had kept the drop cloth on Noor's head to avoid blood spilling all over the robes. We undressed her and I quickly put everything on over my clothes. She had been shorter than me, so the clothes barely covered my ankles, but if I slouched like Noor usually did, I could conceal the hem of my pants. I instantly felt hot from being cloaked in thick black robes, or maybe it was from the adrenaline rushing through my veins.

I eyed the woman's feet, enclosed by worn-out sandals. I grabbed them off her feet and quickly slipped them onto mine. Old shoes were better than no shoes, especially if I had to travel by foot soon.

We ran out of the closet, shutting the door behind ourselves, and resumed our positions at the garage door waiting for the guard. Not a second later, the guard opened the door for us. My heart was beating so fast that I feared he would hear it through my layers of clothes, but he barely gave me a second look. I followed Salena's lead and took a seat next to her in the white minivan in front of us.

We pulled out of the stone-laden garage and onto narrow streets. I kept my head down for the entire ride to conceal my eyes. My eyes were a noticeable shade of green, and if the guard saw them, he'd instantly recognize me. I was unable to see anything with my gaze focused on my tightly balled up hands in my lap and black fabric blocking my periphery. The van jostled us around as we traveled over the bumpy road. The air conditioning wasn't on, so I was sweating profusely under my layers of clothing. Luckily, the blood on my cheek had begun to coagulate and I didn't have to deal with more of it gushing out under the stifling cloth.

We drove for about twenty minutes before coming to an abrupt stop. The guard jumped out of the car and opened the door to let us out.

"I will wait for you here. Be back in forty-five minutes," he warned me gruffly. I didn't look up or speak to him. I simply kept my gaze low and nodded my head in agreement.

In front of us stood a stone path of stairs. It was the longest path I had ever seen. It would take us at least a half hour to climb all those stairs. It led all the way up to a grand white building with what looked like thick, pointed arrows sticking out of the roof.

"Come on. We need to hurry if we're going to make it up there in time," Salena whispered to me without moving her head so the guard wouldn't know she was talking. I could feel his eyes on our backs.

We started up the steps, walking at a brisk pace. I was glad that I had swiped a pair of shoes. Otherwise, the hike would have been impossible on all this uneven stone.

After several minutes of intense climbing, finally where no other visitors were near us, Salena spoke. "Once we make it inside of the building, you can leave through the back exit. There'll be a steep hill that you'll need to get down."

"No stairs?" I was out of breath from trying to keep up with her pace.

"No. It's just a dirt hill with trees. You'll have to climb down. There are a lot of trees, so they should block you from anyone who might be looking."

"Where do I go from there?" We had discussed the plan already, but now I felt completely unprepared, like I was already forgetting the rest of it.

Thankfully, Salena was patient with me. She had everything riding on the success of our plan too. "Once you get to the road, you'll need to make a left and follow along as it winds until you reach Mount Road. Mongoose Inc. should be on that road. If I remember correctly, it's across the street from a sweet shop with a tent, if it's still in business."

I nodded, trying to memorize everything she had just said. "Got it."

We made it in record time to the entrance of the temple. A large bell hovered over the entryway. Salena removed her shoes and rang the bell, then pressed her palms together in prayer.

I looked at her expectantly for further instruction.

"Leave now," she whispered. "If you come inside, you'll have to leave your shoes behind. Follow the wall of the temple and go down the hill."

I nodded and turned to leave the entrance.

"Good luck," she whispered.

"I'll see you soon. I promise."

"I know," she replied walking deeper into the temple and eventually out of my line of sight.

I walked quickly along the outer perimeter of the temple like she had instructed. Luckily, there weren't many visitors along my way. Most seemed like tourists who were just as unfamiliar with the place as I was, so they didn't pay any attention to me. Thankfully, no one looked at me suspiciously for wearing an Islamic *burkah* in a Hindu temple.

The temple covered so much land and had even more land around it. If I hadn't been using it as an escape portal, I would have actually thought this place was serene and loved to explore it some more.

I finally reached the far end of the temple. Looking down the hill in front me, I felt my stomach twist in knots. I was so high up that I felt like I was on a playground swing, swinging too high for comfort.

Instead of looking down all that way below me, I stared at my feet and started moving. If I just focused on my steps, I could do this.

The terrain was so uneven, and I kept tripping on rocks. Salena was right, there were a lot of trees and brush to hide me from view, but I had to pay attention to where I was going before I ran into branches.

I could see the road in the distance packed with rickshaws and cars and even pedestrians walking on the side. I decided to turn left through the brush instead of going all the way down to the road; I would be in plain sight if I didn't stay under the cover of the trees. I followed along, running even as branches caught on my robes. I didn't know how long I would have to keep going before I saw the sign for Mount Road, and it was difficult to see because the *burkah* kept slipping over my eyes. I had to keep readjusting it just to see properly.

The road suddenly split into two. I couldn't see any signs either. *Shit.* Salena hadn't mentioned that the road would fork, so I didn't know which route to take. If I went right, I'd probably end up deep in a thicket of forest. The leftward path was more exposed and seemed to be busier. However, the probability of it leading to a city was higher.

I decided on left.

The road was so bursting with vehicles that I could weave through the stand-still traffic. I slowed my pace so as not to stand out. The smog from the cars was unbearable and suffocating, causing me to gasp for air.

I walked for what felt like a mile in the chaotic street. It was bustling with life, vastly different from the dungeon back at Tarun's palace. Women were dressed in colorful fabrics and talking loudly and even laughing. Men operated various food stands and tried selling their treats to anyone who walked nearby. The air smelled like cloves, cinnamon, and fried dough.

My stomach growled at the assault of scents on my nose. After eating porridge for so long, I was starving. My primal instinct kicked in and I followed my nose, letting the aromas lead me. I had no money and didn't even speak the language, so I wasn't able to eat anything, but my stomach wouldn't let me stray from finding food. I was like a rodent prowling for crumbs.

I came to a stop in front of a small modest, storefront. In the window, there was a case of various snacks. I had no idea what anything was, but I was sure the heavenly smell was coming from this location. I eyed something that looked like a mini funnel cake with syrup or honey slathered all over it. The warm orange color of the coils made my mouth water in excitement. I was so hungry, but I couldn't do anything about it. Tears threatened to fall from my eyes as I turned away from the store front.

My impending emotional breakdown was interrupted by the noisy flapping of fabric overhead. I looked up to find that one end of the tent above me was ripped and slapping against the metal post that held it up.

A tent. I was at a sweet shop with a tent. Was this the same one Salena had been talking about? My mind was racing. I searched the opposite side of the street. *Mongoose Inc.* Staring at me was a hand-painted sign in front of a rundown building. The walls were gray with soot and dirt. I made it!

Forgetting my stomach, I crossed the road. I stared up at the sign in disbelief. I looked around to see if I could see anyone surveilling the building. I didn't know many of Shyam's men, but I was hoping to spot someone I might recognize. I didn't see anyone around.

Turning to the building again, I noticed a camera located at the top corner of the entrance to the building. I had no doubt it belonged to Tarun and his camp was watching me at this very moment.

I moved quickly, before I wouldn't have this chance again. I tore the *burkah* off my head to expose my face and turned away from the building. My red hair, freckled face, and green eyes were on full display to any of Shyam's men who might have been hiding out and capturing photos of trespassers. I stood still for a full thirty seconds to ensure at least one good photo was taken and would strike a hit on the software.

Then I bolted to the side of the building. I didn't know where else to go, so I figured it was best to hide out somewhere nearby in case anyone came looking for me.

As I ran down the alley, I heard shoes slapping against the ground behind me. Tarun had found me.

I ran faster looking for any crevice in the alley to duck into to escape the person behind me. My lungs were about to explode from exertion and my legs were ready about to give out, but I couldn't stop.

The footsteps grew louder with each second that passed by. Something grabbed the back of my clothes and pulled me backward. I slammed into something hard. I was just about scream when a cloth covered my nose and mouth tightly, suffocating me. The hand pressed so hard against my face that the cut on my cheek seared with pain.

I struggled against the hard wall behind me, but something held my waist down from. I couldn't believe I had been so close to escaping and eventually rescuing Salena. I had failed her. I had failed myself.

My vision started to go hazy and I felt my body start to go limp, from my toes all the way up to my chest. My eyelids felt heavy with sleep. Everything around me blurred and then went black.

Chapter XII

Amelia

I came to, the fog from my head slowly clearing and the realization of what had happened settling in. *One of Tarun's goons got me.* My eyes darted around the room. This wasn't my cell. I wasn't back in the dungeon.

I was lying on a wooden bench, unbound and ungagged. I pushed up to sit slowly, taking in my surroundings. I was in some sort of a broken-down warehouse. There weren't any windows at eye level for me to see clearly, only small ones just below the ceiling that barely brought in any sunlight. Electrical wiring in the walls was exposed and the beams holding the ceiling up looked worn down and seconds away from caving in.

A deep voice broke through the residual grogginess, snapping me to attention. I wasn't alone.

I looked over to where the voice was coming from and saw the back of a tall figure. He didn't look like one of Tarun's men, who were usually stocky and unkempt in their clothes. This figure wore a fitted black t-shirt and camouflage cargo pants. He held his spine with perfect posture as he pressed a phone to his ear. He looked like a soldier reporting to his general.

"Yeah, she's here with me. She tried to run." He paused for a moment, giving the other person a chance to respond.

"You should have warned me she was fast," he said next, chuckling into the phone.

"Don't worry. I sedated her just enough to carry her without a fight. Didn't want to make her too hungover to talk. I'll question her when she comes to."

No wonder I felt so out of it. Tarun and his guys must have had stockpiles of sedatives, judging from how much they'd used on me up until this point. I was still confused about why he hadn't handcuffed or gagged me. I could easily run or scream right now, but he'd probably catch me and subsequently punish me for it. Instead, I stayed quiet, listening to the man speak in case he said anything useful for me to use later.

"No, she was alone. Lots of cuts on her feet and a pretty bad gash on her cheek."

I touched my cheek, remembering the cut I had dug into as a way to distract the guard so I could flee my cell.

Bandages. Why would my captor have dressed my wound? Tarun certainly hadn't cared about it after he sliced into my skin. I was sure the thing was infected by now from the lack of care it received.

After a few moments of listening to his boss on the other end, the man spoke again. "Okay. I'll wait here for Jai's call."

Jai? Why would Jai be calling Tarun's man? Unless—

He was about to hang up when I jumped off the bench— too fast for my legs to work properly. I tumbled to the ground, knocking my elbow on the bench with a thud on my way down.

The man turned to check on the commotion I had caused. His eyebrow hitched as he studied me.

"Looks like someone's awake," he said in a low voice into the phone, as if narrating what he was seeing.

My nerves rattled inside. I strained to raise my voice loud enough to be heard; instead, it came out hoarse and shaky. "Is that Shyam?" Uttering his voice aloud was enough to stop my heart from beating just so I could hear his reply clearly.

He stared back at me without replying. His silence was my confirmation.

He hesitated for a beat, listening to *him* on the other line. "Boss wants to talk to you."

He held the phone out to me, and I grabbed it desperately. I had so many things I wanted to say to Shyam—so many things

I wanted to hear in reply. I wanted to tell him about how they took me from my office. How they drugged me and delivered me all the way to Tarun's doorstep. I wanted to tell him how they locked Salena and me into cells and abused us. I wanted to apologize for ruining his business by diverting his shipments. And most of all, I wanted to tell him that I thought of him every day while I was held captive and prayed to be in his arms again. Yet, I couldn't get my voice to start.

He spoke first. "*Jaan.*"

My heart stilled hearing my nickname again. After so many weeks of being held against my will, hearing that familiar deep voice call out for me untied all the knots of anxiety that I had been carrying inside all this time. All the feelings I had locked up tight into a box in order to survive came rushing out of me like water from a burst dam. The dam had crumbled to pieces, tumbling down to the earth. The freed water gushed out of my body as tears when I heard that one beautiful word.

I tasted the saltiness of the streams running down my face on my tongue as I opened my mouth to speak. "Shyam." I sobbed violently, my shoulders shaking uncontrollably.

The line went silent except for what sounded like heavy breaths desperately trying to steady themselves. Then I heard a final leaden exhale on the other end before he spoke again. "Are you okay?"

No. I wasn't. I wanted to tell him everything they had done to me. But there would be time for that later.

I took a deep breath to settle my tears. "Shyam, we have to get Salena. Tarun's keeping her prisoner." I told him how I had escaped and how Tarun was planning to marry Salena tomorrow at his house. I also told him that he was living undercover at his house.

"I know about the wedding," he said. "He's invited my ex-clients and is planning to make a spectacle of it."

"He'll know she had something to do with my escape. Please, you have to get her out of there before he kills her!" I pled. They had probably already discovered that Noor and I were missing by now. Once they found her body, Tarun would put it all together and would take his rage out on Salena.

"We will, *jaan.* In the meantime, I need you to stay with Zayn."

I looked over to the man keeping a watchful eye over me.

"But—I can help! I know the layout of the palace, and—"

"Amelia. No," he cut me off before I could even argue my case. His tone told me that he wasn't up for negotiating on the matter.

I was furious that he thought me incapable of helping. I had been ripped away from all that I knew and treated heinously as a prisoner in another country. I had survived and even escaped, using my own wits. And now he was treating me like a delicate flower, afraid that I would wilt at the slightest change of climate.

"Stop treating me like I'm fragile. I won't break. I made it this far. I promised Salena I'd go back for her."

He sighed, exasperated. "I lost you once and now I need you to stay safe," he said. "Please understand." His tone was different, not one of control and anger. No. This was the sound of a man who was lacking control. He sounded like he had experienced a reckoning of his own power and realized that there was much that was beyond it.

I heard the desperation in his voice. I understood what it was like to not have control over a situation. I had none of it when I was Tarun's prisoner. I wouldn't fight him on this any longer, so I gave in. "Okay."

"I promise I will see you soon, *jaan*." His voice was thankful that I had conceded.

He didn't hang up immediately. Neither of us wanted to be the first to leave so soon after finally being reunited.

I whispered into the phone, "I need you to stay safe, too." He was about to face Tarun, and anything could happen to him. I was lucky to have made it away alive, but he might not be so lucky. Tarun wouldn't let him go without one of them dying in the process.

"I will," he promised, and I believed him.

The phone went dead on the other end.

CHAPTER XIII

SHYAM

I t was difficult to hang up on her, but more difficult to stay on the line—to hear her voice and not be in the same room as her. To listen to her story. To heal her wounds. To console her.

When my phone alerted me that the recognition software had found a match against one of Amelia's photos, I wanted to drive over to her and get her myself. Even though I was in a hotel in Jaipur, it would have been a good twenty minutes before I reached her. Luckily, Zayn had been staked out in an apartment across the street from Mongoose Inc. He had received the notification as soon as I did and acted quickly. He was able to retrieve her and take her to a safe space to hideout.

He had given her a low dose of chloroform to knock her out so she wouldn't resist him. She had nearly evaded him, but her physical strength was no match for Zayn's muscular physique.

He reported a huge gash on her cheek that had been open and wet with coagulated blood. Fortunately, he was able to tend to her wound while she was out cold, before infection set in.

I paced around my hotel room listening to Zayn's report. I balled my fist tightly against my side when he told me the details of her wound. Tarun had done this to her beautiful face. He marked her—caused her pain. I would make his death slow and painful for laying a finger on Amelia. It was my vow to her.

I had already known about Tarun's wedding to Salena. One of our ex-clients had been followed by Javed. He was a distributor from England who had traveled to India for vacation. The guys saw him out at a local bar the night we set-up headquarters at the hotel in Jaipur.

The days of planning had been long. The men needed to let off some steam. They hadn't rested since Amelia had been taken. While I was wasting away in my bed, they had been out working with Jai to locate Tarun and get revenge on my behalf. I felt that they deserved a night off before resuming our work. I let them go out and stayed behind with Jai to refine my plans.

When the guys were out, they overhead one of my former clients, a man named Jameson from England bragging about attending a lavish wedding, referring to it as "the wedding of the year." He had always been loud and boisterous when he was my client. When I was in England for business, he'd insist on holding meetings at the most extravagant restaurants and clubs, always making a scene and flaunting his money. It was distasteful to witness. I was told that he was no different when my men saw him.

Javed remembered his face and kept eyes and ears on him throughout the evening. He never mentioned that it was Tarun's wedding but did spill that it was at a palace in Jaipur that no one had ever been inside near Chandni Road. He flaunted that it was a new business partner to anyone who would listen, making no effort to keep his volume low.

Our ex-clients who had defected to Tarun's side were also invited. They were most likely excited because none of them had seen Tarun in years; he had been undercover all this time to ultimately take over my business. Now that he had, he was about to reveal himself to the world. It was more of a coming-out party than a wedding.

Javed followed the show-off to the bathroom and chloroformed him from behind, then he quickly injected a tracker into his arm and slipped out of the bar, taking the rest of our men with him. All our men carried spare trackers with them just for situations like this where they needed real-time locations.

They gave Jai and I a full report on what happened as soon as they arrived back at the hotel. Jai activated the tracker through his makeshift lab in the living area of his suite. He pulled up the software and found that he was on the move to a hotel nearby to the bar.

We had just found our personal invite to "the wedding of the century."

Chapter XIV

Amelia

I couldn't sleep much that night. Zayn had tried to make the hideout as comfortable as possible, setting out a sleeping bag for me. There weren't any other rooms for him to sleep in, so he slept upright on the bench that I had first found myself lying on when I woke here.

Although he was a stranger to me, my intuition told me that he wouldn't hurt me—especially if he valued his life. He had cared for the gash on my cheek and tended to the cuts on my feet with care. I trusted that Shyam would only send his most trustworthy man to keep an eye on me. It wasn't Zayn that gave me the anxiety nagging at me.

As I tried to sleep in the dark on the factory floor, listening to Zayn's steady breathing, thoughts swam erratically in my mind. Tomorrow, Shyam would infiltrate Tarun's palace, which was to be filled with the some of the most lethal criminals in the world. Rescuing Salena wouldn't be an easy feat and killing Tarun would be even more difficult.

Logically, I knew the odds were against Shyam. No matter how large his army was, Tarun's would be bigger and stronger now that he had secured the allegiance of Shyam's clients. Shyam's men would be outnumbered. I was just hours away from possibly being reunited with him, and it could be taken away from me if he didn't make it out of there alive.

When I arrived at Tarun's doorstep, I had feared I would never see Shyam again. Now, knowing that he was in the same city and I couldn't reach him pained me more.

I was nervous about saving Salena. I had promised her that I would come back for her. If it weren't for her, I wouldn't have been able to escape, so I needed to get her out of there.

I couldn't help but wonder what would happen when Shyam rescued her. Would he feel anything deeper than the nostalgic loyalty he held for her? She clearly still had feelings for him. Perhaps, since things hadn't ended well between them, she still needed closure, so for her there was still something left to the relationship. Shyam said that he was over her, but maybe seeing his ex-fiancée in person and rescuing her from captivity might ignite the sparks that had once burned. The jealously I had once held for their relationship festered inside me anew since I now had the chance to dwell on them.

Shyam didn't want me near the wedding when he launched his attack against Tarun. I knew the palace better than him or any of his men, so I was frustrated that he wouldn't accept my help. I understood his reasons, because they were the same reasons that I had for wanting to be with him right now. He wanted me safe. However, I was still on edge.

My impatience replaced any logical sense I had. I wanted to leave the factory to be with him. I kicked restlessly under the covers of my sleeping bag. My legs were ready to run to take me to him. My brain was on high alert to direct me there. But I had to wait.

I took a deep breath, allowing the musky air in the dilapidated building to draw down my windpipe and inflate my lungs with air. I exhaled slowly, allowing my breaths to steady my heartrate. The cyclic rise and fall of my chest stilled my mind just briefly enough to allow drowsiness to make my eyelids heavy. I let sleep take over in the hopes that the night would pass quickly, bringing me closer to reuniting with the man I had dreamed of while I was in hell.

**

"Wake up, Sleeping Beauty."

I squinted my eyes open to see Zayn standing over me. He was dressed like he was attending a gala, in a tailored shirt and slacks, except with all forms of weaponry strapped to various parts of his body. He no doubt had a muscular body underneath all that gear that was probably as deadly as any weapon he carried.

"What time is it?" I rubbed my eyes as I sat up.

"Nine o'clock. I figured you needed some extra sleep to help your body recover." He seemed genuinely concerned about me. He had one of those faces that you could trust.

I fingered the bandage on my cheek. "Thanks."

The grogginess reminded me of exactly how much my body had endured over the past weeks. I hadn't slept much except for being drugged anytime Tarun's, or Shyam's, men deemed fit. The soreness of my muscles screamed at me to go back to sleep and get more rest.

He passed me something rolled up in wax paper that looked like it might have been a burrito. "I got you some breakfast."

My stomach growled at the mention of the word "breakfast" as I took the package from him. Folding back the paper allowed aromas of spices and butter to invade my nose. I greedily bit into the soft flour wrap. The hearty taste of cheese and a spicy yet savory sauce made my taste buds crave another bite.

Zayn chuckled. "That good?"

"Mmmmmhmmm," I managed as I stuffed some more into my mouth. "What is this?" I asked with my mouth full. I knew it wasn't polite, but I was too hungry to be concerned with niceties.

"Paneer in roti."

Cheese in bread. I was familiar with Indian food from living in Seattle and New York. Both cities had a large Indian community, so I ate at Indian restaurants often. I had ordered paneer tikka masala often. I loved the way the cheese was cut into large cubes and simmered in gravy. I had always opted for naan before, but I had never had Indian bread that was so thin and flaky before. It was delicious how it melted in my mouth.

"What type of roti is this?" I asked, having already consumed half of the roll.

"Parantha," he answered.

"I don't think I've ever had this before. It's so good."

"I'm glad you like it. It's from a stand not too far from here. I bought two in case you wanted another." He held out the bag.

I could have eaten another, but I knew I would be sick if I tried to scarf it down since I hadn't eaten much while in captivity. My stomach wasn't used to having anything this rich. "No, thanks. Did you eat?"

He smiled, seemingly touched that I was concerned about him in return. "Yes." He went back to checking his guns for ammunition before strapping more to his body.

It seemed like a lot for just hiding out in the safe space. "Are you going somewhere?"

"Tarun's wedding," he said without looking up at me as he secured his tailored vest to his chest to cover his weapons.

I jumped up to stand, excited to be included. I flinched because although my feet were covered in bandages, they still felt raw when I stood on them. I had changed out of the *shalwar* that Tarun had given me because it was too filthy to wear any longer. I'd opted to just wear Noor's black garb without the face covering, since it was the cleaner option. I didn't have any other clothes to change into, but I was sure it didn't matter. We weren't technically guests at the wedding.

"I'm ready," I said excitedly.

"No." He shook his head, buttoning his suit jacket. "I'm going. You are to stay here."

Anger flowed through my veins, radiating to my extremities. "The hell I am," I shouted.

"Not my rules," he said, unamused by my tantrum. "Boss's order." He went back to packing his bag with various things he'd need for the raid.

"Fuck your boss," I spat with my hands on my hips. It was rude, but I was fed up. I wasn't a child. These past few weeks had proven that I could take care of myself, and if these macho men couldn't see that, then they were idiots.

Zayn left his bag and stood up right. A sly smirk spread across his lips.

"Don't laugh at me! I'm tired of being treated like a kid."

"I didn't mean to make it seem like I was laughing at you. It's just that I'm not used to anyone talking about Shyam that way—well, maybe except for Jai."

"Look, I just want to be involved. Before I came here, Shyam told me that I was a part of the team and I just want to be treated like one."

Zayn considered what I said but didn't respond.

"I know the house better than any of you," I continued. "I know where he keeps Salena in the dungeons. I can be more useful than you all give me credit for."

"Shyam gave me explicit orders to keep you here. He wants you safe."

"I understand his reasons, but your raid will be more successful with me there. I'm not dumb. I was able to outsmart Tarun to tip you all off about my escape," I argued.

"No one is doubting your intelligence and strength, Amelia. It's just too dangerous. There's no guarantee that I'll even come back alive," he said, his face turning serious.

"Please," I begged. "I promise I won't do anything risky. I promised Salena I'd come back for her and I don't want to disappoint her."

He sighed in resignation. I had worn him down. "Okay. You can come. But you stay in the car. You can fill me in on the layout of the house while we drive over there."

Being in the car was better than being left here in the safe space. "Thank you!" I smiled, eager to be on our way.

He shook his head, grabbing his bag off the floor. "Shyam is going to kill me."

"I'll be sure to plan the most extravagant funeral for you, then." I smirked.

He smiled at me, his expression turning light and jovial. "You really are something. Now I see why he loves you."

I stilled at his words. I had heard something similar from his brother a long time ago. I tried to ignore them to avoid any disappointment. They carried no weight unless they came from Shyam himself. But would they ever come straight from him?

CHAPTER XV

SHYAM

Today was the wedding.

I examined myself in the full-length mirror in my hotel suite. I had just stepped out of the shower and wrapped the towel I used to dry my skin low around my waist. Droplets of moisture still coated my skin because I was too focused on my thoughts to dry myself thoroughly. My frame was leaner now; I had lost muscle mass from not working out since Amelia had been taken. The bags under my eyes were deep like valleys. I still refused to shave until she was in my arms again, so the coarse hairs on my jaw had grown long enough to just cover my skin.

I saw my father in my reflection—not the strong man who grew an empire, but the broken shell of a man in the last years of his life after my mother died.

My men usually dressed in fatigues and bulletproof vests for missions. However, we had opted for suits for this occasion. I would be easily noticed by any of my former clients in attendance, but dressing in a suit would allow me to slip by catering staff or wedding planners without standing out if needed. They would assume I was just another guest. I also wanted to send a message to Tarun that I didn't fear him. Amelia was safe and under watch, so he no longer held the upper hand in this war.

I had just set to work on securing my tie when Jai entered my room. He was in slacks and a collared shirt and tie, with no jacket. However, this *was* dressy for him; he had the same idea about blending in as I did.

"Looking sharp."

I eyed his reflection over my shoulder in the mirror as I tightened the knot around my neck.

"You clean up good, too," I said.

"Almost ready to go?" he asked taking a seat on the chair near the bedroom door.

I checked my wrists again to ensure my cufflinks were in place. Satisfied with my appearance, I grabbed my phone from the nightstand and tucked it into my pocket. "Are the men ready?"

"They're armored up and loaded with ammunition. I've tracked Jameson and he arrived at the house on Chandni Road five minutes ago. We've had surveillance confirm that it is, in fact, the site of the wedding."

Until recently, we had no knowledge of the wedding or where it was to take place. We had gotten lucky when Jameson ran his mouth at the bar, allowing Javed to overhear him and place a tracker in him.

"Tarun's no longer hiding the location of his house?" I asked.

"I guess he has no need to. He thinks he won over the empire."

I supposed that was true. He had accomplished everything that he had set out to. He had stolen the women in my life and taken my business. My clients had defected to his side and no one and uttered a word about the wedding or the location to me. If Amelia hadn't planned an escape, we wouldn't have known where Tarun was. He felt confident that he held all the power in this vendetta, and he wanted to make a show of it, with all my ex-clients there to witness it. "He wants us to come."

"It seems so. He's expecting a show on his big day."

Slipping my weapon into the waistband of my pants so that it was concealed by the back of my jacket, I smirked. "Then let's not disappoint him."

***

Jai and I rode separately from our crew, with Saran as our driver. The other vans full of reinforcements rode apart from each other so as not to attract attention on the way. Although Tarun knew we would be there, we wanted to infiltrate his wedding quietly to give an edge.

One van of men headed over before the rest of us posing as wedding venue workers. Indian weddings were large and involved the building of a massive stage called a *mandap* where the ceremony would take place. The stages were usually elaborately designed with heavy vases on the floor and large garlands of flowers draped around the frame. The preparations required a lot of workers, both male and female, to arrange everything perfectly. We chose our leanest men to access the wedding venue first. They had to be unassuming, so sending thick, muscular men would only have raised suspicions.

The batch of our "wedding venue" men reported back to me that they had successfully gained access.

Tarun hadn't yet inspected the ceremony site in the back of his palace, as I was told. He was most likely too busy primping himself for his grand entrance. None of his men suspected anything out of the ordinary either. The guys we sent were younger recruits who hadn't been seen in association with our organization yet. They had been tasked with lacing the venue with explosives, and we knew they had completed the job without error because Jai was able to locate each explosive from his phone. They would detonate at the push of a button from either of our phones.

The venue men had slipped special sedatives into the alcohol to be served at the wedding. Hindu weddings were usually a dry affair, but we were criminals, so none of us ever took that rule seriously except for Tarun, who for some reason never drank. He did, however, have bottles of champagne ready to greet his guests upon arrival. Two of my men used syringes to inject mild sedatives into each of the bottles through the corks. The cases were lined up and ready to be served, so they had to work quickly. The drug wouldn't knock anyone out fully, but it would alter their judgment-making skills enough to not be a threat when shit went down. We didn't want to maim anyone, just throw off their alertness before they came to Tarun's aid. And since Tarun didn't drink, it would be a fair fight when I got him to myself.

The other vans were instructed to wait for the wedding to start before approaching the palace. Everyone would be too preoccupied with the ceremony and directing their attention to Tarun to notice the vehicles approaching the perimeter. It was highly likely that Tarun would have guards stationed out front during the ceremony since he was expecting us and wanted to be notified when were about to infiltrate his palace, so our men were instructed to shoot-to-kill as soon as any of them were spotted. We needed the lead time to get inside before Tarun was tipped off about our arrival.

At least Amelia wasn't being held captive inside. I had instructed Zayn to keep her at the safe space. She was, under no circumstances, allowed to leave. I had originally planned for Zayn to stay with her, but Jai had convinced me that we'd need him to coordinate the men from outside of the venue while we were inside. He would also have permissions to detonate the explosives we planted if Jai and I couldn't do it ourselves. Amelia would be safe under guard watch, so I didn't have to worry about her getting hurt.

Our car stopped just before reaching Chandni Road. We would wait until the festivities began to enter. In Hindu weddings, it was customary for the groom to start the ceremony with rituals of his own before the bride joined him on the *mandap*. We timed everything exactly so we could invade before Salena joined Tarun on the stage with her father. It would be safer to take Tarun down without her present. We would free her after the coast was clear.

The weight of the revenge that lay before us weighed heavily on my shoulders. The Sethi legacy depended on today. Everything had been ripped away from me by this *benchod*. *Sister fucker.* Today, I would get it all back. There was no option to fail and try again later.

"Boss, the ceremony is about to start," Javed said in his gruff voice from the front passenger seat.

"Men in place?" I asked.

"Yes," he replied.

"Zayn's ETA?"

He checked his phone. "Fifteen minutes away."

I looked over to my brother, who waited for my signal. I placed my hand on the handle of my door and pulled until it clicked, opening the door. "Then let's pay our respects to the groom."

Chapter XVI

Amelia

I briefed Zayn on what I remembered of the layout of Tarun's house, paying particular attention to the path to the dungeon. From what he told me of the plans, they were hoping to attack before Salena joined the ceremony. Hopefully, she would be left in the dungeon, safe from any flying bullets or explosions.

It was hot inside of the silver four-door sedan that we rode in to Tarun's house. I placed my hands on the air vents, desperate to feel air.

"It's not on," Zayn said with his eyes trained on the traffic in front of us. Indian roads seemed to always be filled with mopeds, bikes, and pedestrians.

"Does the AC even work?"

"Yes, but the car is old, so I save it for when I really need it," he said, still focusing on the road.

"So…this is *your* car?" I asked, surprised.

"Whose else would it be?"

"I guess I expected you to have something more—showy."

"Are you trying to tell me that you don't like my car?" he teased.

"No, no," I corrected him nervously. Embarrassed that I had put my foot in my mouth, I continued, "I just meant that since you worked with Shyam, I expected you to have something flashy like him. He seems to collect fancy cars like toys from the inside of cereal boxes."

A quizzical expression formed on his face. "Cereal boxes?"

I guess that expression doesn't translate well. "It's an American thing."

"It's my car, but only for when I run missions. It's better to use a car that doesn't stand out when I'm supposed to be unnoticeable. I have other, more *comfortable* cars at home." He smiled.

"Do you live in Punjab too?" I knew it was where Shyam and Jai had their base and I assumed Zayn would live nearby too if he worked for them.

"I do."

"How did you meet Shyam and Jai?" I asked.

"My father worked for their father."

I had no idea their history went that far back. "Oh, wow. Did you always want to follow in your father's footsteps?"

"It's a little more complicated than that," he said. "My father fell on hard times after my mother died when I was younger. He met Shyam's father, who gave him a job and a house. My father ended up becoming his closest employee and we were even treated like family. I grew up with Shyam and Jai and their mother looked after me like I was her own. After my father died, I took over his role for the family."

"You felt indebted to them?" I asked.

"Never. Shyam and Jai are my brothers. It was never even a decision to make. I would always stand by them because they *are* my family."

I admired his loyalty. I could see why Shyam trusted him. He seemed sincere whenever he spoke. The glint that never seemed to disappear from his eye added to his likeable personality. He was built like a warrior but could be warm and approachable when he spoke of things that mattered to him, like the Sethi brothers.

Gazing out my window, I noticed the roads looked familiar. My heartrate spiked as I recognized some of the same pink buildings from when I had been brought here as a prisoner weeks ago.

My breathing increased as my heart dropped into the pit of my stomach. I gripped the handle on the door tightly. My inhales and exhales were audible and blocked out the sounds of the noisy streets.

Zayn must have stopped the car because, before I realized it, both of his hands were on me, shaking my shoulders to get my attention. I couldn't hear his words even though his mouth was moving, so I just focused on his eyes, begging for help. He demonstrated slow inhales through his nose and even slower exhales through his mouth.

I mimicked his motions until the spots in front of my eyes slowly faded and my hearing returned.

"Are you okay?" Zayn said, rubbing small circles on my back to soothe me.

I nodded, unable to speak.

"Have you ever had a panic attack before?"

I shook my head.

"You're okay," he said soothingly. "It's a perfectly normal re-action for someone who is returning to where they were held captive. I shouldn't have brought you here."

I shook my head again and swallowed to clear my throat. "No. I'm okay. Please let me stay."

His phone buzzed. He checked the screen and hurriedly tucked it back into his pocket.

"Fine. But stay in the car," he warned.

"I will," I promised, even though I didn't want to.

He eyed me skeptically, as if wondering whether to trust me. Then, he opened the glove compartment and rummaged through it, searching for something. I noticed the flash of a silver handgun amidst other supplies stored in the tiny compartment. He grabbed a phone and tossed it into my lap before closing the glove compartment.

"A phone?"

"Use this burner phone to text me if anything happens while you're out here. My number is the only one programmed into it."

I checked the contact list to verify. "Okay. Thank you."

"Don't make me regret this," he warned, pointing his finger at me like a father would to his child.

"Why d*id* you bring me?" I asked. He could have just tied me up and left me behind so I would stay put. Instead, I was right outside in the getaway car.

"Because I would do the same thing if I were you. And you would have found a way to follow me." He smiled and exited the car before I had a chance to respond.

There I sat, waiting. Waiting for something to happen. A loud boom from explosions. Screams. Gunfire. But none of those things occurred.

I didn't know if it was the building heat in the stuffy car or because I was outside of my captor's home—the place where I was beaten, slashed, and left in a cell for days—but I felt anxiety creep back into my chest. My diaphragm was taut with tension, preventing me from taking the long inhales and exhales that Zayn had instructed me to use. My breaths came out short and quick, like I was hyperventilating again.

I couldn't stay in the car a moment longer, even though I had promised Zayn I would. I opened the glove compartment and grabbed the gun I had seen.

My hand moved to the latch on the door and pulled. Fresh air invaded my nostrils as I tumbled out. My breathing came easier as soon as I was no longer contained in that tiny car.

I had never had an issue with panic attacks in my life, so I didn't know how to handle these fits I kept experiencing. Perhaps this would be my new normal since I had been a victim of kidnapping. I should probably see a therapist when I reached home, but for now, I needed to do something. Anything but sit still and wait. I couldn't suppress my reaction to being near this house again, so I needed to find another way to satisfy my need for control.

I stood upright and tucked the gun in my waistband. I looked around the street and didn't see anyone in sight. The large security gate in front of the house was open for the wedding. I snuck through the gate without anyone stopping me. I found it odd that no guards were stationed there, especially when the gate was opened to allow guests inside. Perhaps Shyam's men had gotten to the guards already.

Zayn told me that the wedding would most likely be outside, so I was assuming that the guests would need to go through the house to get to the gardens in the back. I couldn't go through the front entrance for fear of being seen, so I quietly snaked around to the side of the pink palace, unsure of where it would take me. I hadn't been able to explore the perimeter to know the layout, so I proceeded with caution.

The exterior of the house was made of stone and the doors were reinforced with steel, leaving it an impenetrable fortress. I was sure the windows would be reinforced to avoid break-ins too, so I decided against trying to break one open with the pebbles that decorated the pathway.

Ducking low to avoid anyone seeing me from inside a window, I continued along the perimeter. A figure caught my eye through one of the windows, and I dropped to the ground on my belly to hide. After taking a few steadying breaths, I peeked up to see if the person had left. The figure seemed to belong to a young woman, most likely a maid. The person didn't seem to have noticed me, to my relief.

An idea came to me. I felt for one of the many pebbles I lay upon. My hand rested on a large, smooth one. I held it in my fist and swung my hand, releasing the stone. It flew from my hand to the window on the first floor, causing a loud *clack* against the glass. Nothing happened. I repeated the motions again with another pebble and then another. The window opened. I slipped my hand under my top, grabbing the gun. I clicked the safety off.

The maid stuck her head out the window, searching for the source of the tapping. Suddenly, she locked eyes on me. I remembered her from my time as a prisoner here. She must have remembered me too. Her eyes widened with alarm and her mouth opened as if to scream for help. I jumped to my feet, closing the distance between us, and aimed the gun to her face. She froze with fear.

I had only killed a person once before, and that was because it was necessary. I didn't want to make a habit of it, but I needed the woman to believe that her life was in danger so she'd stay quiet. From the looks of it, I was very convincing.

I spoke before she could cry for help. "Don't scream."

She pressed her lips together in agreement. She understood English.

"You remember me?"

She nodded, terror keeping her eyelids from blinking.

"I don't want to hurt you," I said shakily.

Her shoulders relaxed slightly upon my admission.

116

"I don't want to hurt you, but I will if you don't help me inside."

She nodded again.

"Help me inside—please." I was on a mission, but I wasn't planning on being a jerk about it.

She remained immobile, as if considering my request. She noticed me grip the gun tighter and extended her hand out the window.

I grabbed on, still clutching the gun in my other hand. I kicked my foot off the wall to give myself extra momentum before stumbling inside.

I stood up quickly, with my gun still at attention. "Thank you."

"You're welcome," she replied, to my surprise.

"Where is Salena?" I asked.

Still eyeing the gun, she said, "The dungeon."

"Then, the wedding hasn't begun?"

"It has. Master must perform his ceremonies first, before his bride joins him to complete the marriage." Her voice was so robotic when she spoke of Tarun. The poor girl had probably been brainwashed by him.

"Please don't scream or run for help. I just want to save Salena." Maybe she knew what a monster her boss was and would sympathize with my cause.

"I want to leave too," she said in a small voice.

"You want to be free?" I had to make sure I understood what she meant.

She nodded. "Yes."

I paused for a moment. I knew what it was like to be here against your own will. I wanted to help anyone who wished to be free from this hell hole.

I would probably regret it, but I pushed the gun toward her. She back away, the fear returning to her face.

"Take it," I said.

She looked even more confused.

"Take the gun and use it to get away."

"I cannot. They will find me." Her brown eyes shone with disappointment. She had pretty features and long, dark hair. She had to have been around my age. The men here probably used her for more than just doing their laundry and serving their food.

"We don't have time for this," I said quickly. "Take it and use it if you need to. Everyone is distracted with the wedding, so you need to leave now if you're ever going to get out of here."

She stared at the gun as if trying to decide. Then she opened her hand so I could place it into her palm.

"The safety is off, so be careful. All you need to do is pull the trigger," I said, pointing to it with my finger.

In the distance, the deep bass of drums sounded.

Tears leaked down her long lashes and onto her cheeks. She stared at me with gratitude.

I understood how she felt, but I had to get going if I was going to get to Salena before the guards did. "Go now."

My stern tone made her move quickly out of the window. She slid out silently and ran toward freedom.

I hoped she would find a better life than the one that had been stolen from her by Tarun.

My pride was short lived when I realized that I was now weaponless in a house full of criminals.

I should have left with her too and waited in the car like I had promised, but it was too late. I was already inside.

The burner phone. I could text Zayn and let him know I was in the house, but I couldn't remember where I left it. My hands swiped desperately over my clothes, feeling for it. *Fuck.* I must have dropped it when I left the car.

Think, Becker! I was already inside, so the best option was to find Salena in the dungeon and pray I found a way to get us both out alive. I had promised that I would come back for her, and I wouldn't leave her behind again.

The room I was in resembled a bedroom of some sort. It didn't look lavish enough to be Tarun's room. It was bare, with just a mattress on the floor. I was betting it belonged to one of his servants, maybe even the maid I had just freed, whose name I'd never know.

I made my way across the room to the door. I put my hand on the knob and took in a big breath to prepare myself for my mission—

The knob turned without my wrist rotating it. In one quick motion, the door swung open and I jumped back, startled.

My eyes met a towering ogre of a man. I remembered this guard. His lips parted into a lecherous smile displaying crooked teeth, like he had won a jackpot prize.

"Couldn't stay away, *ladkee*?" he said, cackling. He found my fear amusing, drawing closer to me.

I backed away, trying to evade his proximity. My back hit the wall behind me, next to the open window that the maid had used to escape.

The man with the crooked smile glanced at the window. "How did you manage to open the window? These are locked tight from the inside," he barked at me, his hands pinning my shoulders to the wall.

I couldn't tell him about the maid. He'd send someone after her. If one of us was going to survive, I'd rather it be her. Instead, I opted for vagueness. "I have my ways."

The barrel of a gun pressed against my temple. I shuddered at its cool touch.

"Smart-mouth bitch. Boss will be glad to have you back. He's been looking for you." He wrapped his hand around the back of my neck, giving it a tight squeeze before yanking me forward.

Chapter XVII

Shyam

The wedding had already begun when we entered the premises. Jai and I were able to make a quiet entrance through the back of the venue as we took our spots near the catering staff, who were busy preparing the food. No one noticed us on our way in since the ceremony was already underway. Everyone was preoccupied with the rituals taking place on the stage. The guests and some of Tarun's men were successfully inebriated from the mild sedative in the drinks they had received upon arrival.

The courtyard was decorated beautifully. One wouldn't have been able to tell this was the wedding of a psychopath with a criminal audience. Over-the-top arrangements of flowers in large gold containers dotted each row along both sides of the aisle. My traitorous ex-clients were dressed in their best clothes for the event, all glued to their seats. Some were in traditional Indian wear while others opted for suits, like Jai and me.

The *mandap*, or covering, was decorated with flowers and leaves, mimicking the style of the arrangements down the aisle. Lush bundles of white Indian jasmine adorned each corner of the *mandap*. The sweet fragrance lingered in the air and trailed to even the furthest reaches of the venue.

The aisle was covered in an intricate design made of brightly colored flower petals waiting for the bride to make her appearance. It was customary for Indian brides to make their entrance later in the ceremony with their parents, so it was not time for Salena to arrive yet. My men had successfully located her father in the palace and were given instructions to finish him off. Hopefully, this shit would be taken care of before the guard went to retrieve Salena.

Tarun was more than happy with being the center of attention in the meantime. The priest recited various prayers as the groom sat on a small bench in front of the *hawan*, or fire. He looked nothing like the chubby teenager that I had seen in his photos. His short body was adorned by a deep-red jacket. Emerald jewels and pearls that were heavily encrusted into the fabric shined bright from the stage. Even at the back of the room with my sunglasses on, I could see them glinting in the sunlight. I had no doubt they were real stones and not the fake ones that were usually stitched onto bridal wear. The entire venue knew he had money, but it wasn't enough. He had to make a show of it to anyone who would pay him attention.

Tarun was busy performing the rituals as the priest instructed. Even with something as simple as making offerings to the small alter in front of him, he accomplished it with a flourish. This was the most theatrical performance of his life—marrying his biggest enemy's former fiancée and taking control of the remains of his empire. He treated it as if he were the new king of the underworld and this was his coronation. *Over my dead fucking body.*

From my periphery, I could see Zayn take his place off to the side. He didn't look my way and acknowledge me to keep up the façade that he was part of the wedding crew. I was glad to have him by my side along with Jai—my brothers whom I trusted completely. Thankfully, Amelia was safe out of harm's way under guard watch.

I returned my gaze to the stage. Tarun was pouring water on the alter to complete another ritual. He relished in the attention, lifting the small clay pot high into the air to allow the stream of water to flow. Unfortunately, when the water hit the alter, it splashed the priest off to the side. He really was crazy.

"He's loving the attention," Jai murmured to me while still facing the stage.

"Let him enjoy it," I replied. "His time is running out." We were ready. I balled my hands into fists at my sides, preparing myself for what was about to come.

Jai covertly pulled his phone out, waiting for my signal. His finger hovered over the button to detonate.

My gaze focused on my target under the *mandap*. I nodded my head once before Jai's finger made contact with the button.

BOOM.

The first bomb went off, sending flowers and shards of clay from the containers that held them flying in the air. Screams blared around the courtyard. Tipsy guests did their best to scramble to their feet, shoving each other in a hoard of chaos to escape for safety.

BOOM.

Another explosion. The crowd was a stumbling mess, crashing into tables and blocking Tarun's men from running to their boss's aid. Their judgment was skewed, so they were bewildered as to what was happening. They were clearly drunk themselves, their reaction times slower than what would be expected.

As the venue emptied of guests and workers, my line of sight to the stage cleared. Tarun was huddled in the corner of the stage as three of his men lined up in front of him with their weapons drawn and aimed, ready to fire. He cowered in fear like the pussy that he was. He knew we would be making an appearance, but the explosions had scared him so much that he did what he knew best—hide.

More of his men ran to the stage to protect their master as soon as they were freed from the crowds rushing out. This was working out better than we had planned. All that were left were the two armies and their commanders.

When the smoke cleared from the explosions and all fell silent in the courtyard, Tarun straightened up and caught my stare. Recognition dawned on his face. With one look, he knew the cause of the explosions at his wedding. He continued to stare down his nose at me as his men moved in formation alongside him.

My men followed suit, forming lines on the battlefield behind me. To my right was Jai and to my left was Zayn, both with guns in hand. I had yet to draw my weapon as a show of my power. Guns would be necessary in a moment, but right now, words needed to be had.

"Ah, the Sethi brothers. I see you still know how to make an entrance," he said and snickered.

"I see you still know how to hide like a bitch," Jai retorted, spitting the venom he had been holding in for years.

"You call it 'hiding,' I call it 'luring the snake out of *their* hole.' And what a fancy hole it is—that company you run in New York. It's like you almost forgot your petty roots from your trashy mother."

Jai started toward the stage, ready to rip Tarun to shreds for speaking against our mother. I put my arm out to stop him, not taking my eyes off the enemy.

"Oh, did I upset baby Sethi?" Tarun sneered, his tone making a mockery of my brother. "Your mother was a whore. She proved it by taking our dicks repeatedly. She could go hours without tiring—the mark of a seasoned harlot." He rubbed his hand over his crotch, as if reliving memories. It made me want to wretch where I stood.

I felt Jai's hold on my forearm tighten with rage. I grabbed his wrist and squeezed it before letting go to warn him not to react hastily. Tarun was baiting us and we couldn't give in. We needed to maintain the upper hand and remain clearheaded.

"I'm afraid you've wasted your time today, gentlemen," Tarun said, waving his wrist in the air as if he were the Queen of England shooing us away because he was bored. "I already own the empire and nothing you can do can reverse that. You lost."

"That remains to be seen," I said, my voice echoing through the courtyard as I removed my sunglasses and placed them in my jacket pocket.

"You have never been one for optimism, Shyam. What has changed? Oh—I know. 'Love,' is it?" He danced back and forth, joining his thumb with the rest of his fingertips in the air as if he were tying an imaginary bow out of ribbon.

He was referring to Amelia. Thank God she was safe and away from this nut job.

I kept my expression flat, not showing any emotion at his reference to the only thing that mattered to me.

"I have to say, your girl is a smart one. Wherever did you find her?" He stepped closer to the edge of the stage, cocking his head to one side.

Amelia was my trigger, and if he didn't stop pressing, I would lose it. "Cut the shit, Tarun. You know why we're here. Surrender yourself."

One of his men whispered something to him. His lips slowly spread into a devious smile—the kind that signaled nothing good. "Looks to me like I still hold all of the cards."

Zayn tightened his hold on his rifle, shifting slightly in his spot. Tarun glanced at him. "Drop your weapons and I'll consider leniency."

Not a chance. "It's too late for negotiations," I said. There was no way he was getting away this time.

His smile widened, showing teeth. He clasped his hands in front of his chest in excitement, like a child in front of a Christmas tree. "From the way I see it, it's never too late to negotiate." He stared off to the side.

A guard came forward, dragging a disheveled woman by a chain around her neck. The woman struggled forward as she was yanked along, her feet unsteady on the ground. Oily red hair formed a curtain covering most of her face. *No.*

My heart stopped as I searched for a hint of her face to prove my theory wrong. *Please, God. No.*

The guard yanked on the chain once more and stopped moving abruptly. The woman fell to the floor, her hands breaking her fall. He cursed at her and moved behind her, pulling her upright by the hair on the back of her head. Her head tilted upward from the pain, revealing the face that had haunted my dreams so many nights. *Amelia.*

"Fuck," Jai whispered.

Blood roared through my veins, rushing through my ears, closing me off from the world and trapping me in this nightmare. Her green eyes, full of terror, found mine as I stared back in disbelief. Tears stained her face, more evident with the film of dirt that coated her cheeks. I saw the bandage that covered the gash that Zayn had informed me of.

My sweet Amelia. How the fuck had it come to this? She was supposed to be safe, far away from this battleground. Rage pulsed through my body, tensing my muscles.

128

"Let her go," I bellowed.

Tarun burst into laughter. The maniacal cackle echoed through the courtyard, slicing the tension surrounding our men.

My limbs moved like springs, jolting forward toward her.

"Move and she dies!" Tarun screamed. The guard followed his command and pressed his gun to the side of her head.

I froze in place, the threat in front of me too real to ignore. She pressed her lips together tightly to muffle her cries. Any sounds from her would have just urged Tarun's hand to punish her.

I locked eyes with her, silently promising to get her out of this alive, even though I wasn't sure of it myself.

Somehow, Jai had ended up behind me and put a hand on my back to steady me.

"I can see why you care about this one," Tarun continued. I moved my attention to him as he stepped off the stage and approached Amelia, moving slowly on purpose to build my anxiety. He was unpredictable and would do anything if it meant torturing me.

He ran the back of his finger down her cheek over her bandage. He must have applied too much pressure because she winced from the pain. My muscles twitched, ready to strike. Jai must have sensed it because he squeezed my shoulder as a reminder to control myself.

"Skin so soft—like an angel." Suddenly, Tarun ripped the bandage off, causing her to cry out. "It's too bad she misbehaves often. She's lucky she has me to keep her in line." He pushed his face closer to hers. "I'm sorry I had to mar you, but you needed to be taught a lesson. Your former master didn't do a good job at breaking you in, did he?"

I could see how deep her wound was from where I stood. My stomach roiled. The motherfucker had sliced clean into her cheek. There was no way this would heal on its own. She needed stitches.

Tarun looked over his shoulder toward me, "You seem shocked, Shyam. Didn't she tell you that I own her now?"

I continued to glare at him, waiting to strike.

"Amelia, sweetheart, you didn't tell him about your time with me?" He chuckled.

I stared in confusion. His riddles were getting to me and I couldn't figure out their meaning.

"It was the most glorious of times. I've never known a more supple cunt—so tight yet wet for me." He resumed stroking her skin, moving his hand down her neck, stopping just between her breasts. She was shaking so hard, it looked like she was having a small seizure.

The blood from my head drained and my gut turned with nausea. He had forced himself on her!

"I've had my dick in her, spilling my seed inside to erase all trace of you. I've tasted her nectar, and I'll let you know a little secret…she tastes better than your mother."

I launched toward the stage, ready to rip him apart. I wouldn't stop until his blood soaked the ground he stood on.

BANG. BANG.

Two gunshots fired, followed by Amelia's scream, stopped my feet mid-sprint. Her face fixed into a sob, she stared in horror at something over my shoulder. I turned to see a woman in an ornate Indian dress sprawled out on the floor. *Salena.* Red silk draped over her body and flowed onto the floor in the same manner as the blood spilling from her chest, making it difficult to discern the fabric from the blood on the ground. Jewels from her dress and on her body sparkled as she lay lifeless, making her look almost angelic. *A sleeping angel.*

My eyes immediately flashed to the gun next to her body. She had tried to kill Tarun, but his guard got to her first. Her last moments in life were spent trying to rid the world of the mess that we men had made.

BANG.

Another gunshot fired, this time into the courtyard, shattering a flower arrangement inches from my head. A symphony of shots sounded behind me from our side. This was it. Our armies charged each other, clashing in the middle of the battleground. Gun in hand, I charged the stage with eyes only for my nemesis.

131

CHAPTER XVIII

AMELIA

Men rushed each other on the field. I was no longer able to see Shyam in the chaos. I wriggled against the guard to free myself so I could move in closer to find him, but he squeezed me tighter.

I could barely make out Jai and Zayn in the sea of men and bullets. Jai was facing off with a guard, back handing him with his gun across the face. The guard fell to the ground, but before he could get up, Jai fired two shots into the center of his forehead, then turned to tackle another of Tarun's guards running toward him head-on.

Zayn was a warrior, fending off two men at the same time with a swift combination of kicks and punches that seemed to flow from him like a rehearsed martial arts routine. Although

Tarun's men were capable opponents, they weren't a match for Zayn's skilled combat.

I heard commotion coming from the direction of the stage. Shyam had a gun in his hand, ready to fire, when Tarun barreled into him. They tumbled to the floor, sending the gun skittering out of arm's reach. Tarun sunk his teeth into the side of Shyam's neck like a rabid dog, causing Shyam to cry out from the pain. I screamed as Tarun released his hold on Shyam's flesh and smiled through the blood smeared on his lips. My stomach turned at the sight before me. Tarun's eyes were crazed, like the blood only fueled his need for more. He stretched over Shyam and grabbed the fallen gun, then turned swiftly and aimed it between Shyam's eyes.

"No!" I cried. I pulled against the guard's hold, frantically trying to get away.

"Stay still, whore," he shouted, struggling to hold me with how violently I resisted. When I only fought harder, he knocked me on the back of my head with something hard, stunning me.

I fell to the ground, spots dancing in front of my eyes. In a daze, I rolled around, trying to get my eyes to focus. Gunshots mixed with the sounds of hand-to-hand combat filled my ears as I regained my vision. A shadow towering over me came into focus. As my eyesight sharpened, I could see the guard aiming his weapon at me.

"You've been nothing but trouble since the day you came here," he seethed. "I'm going to enjoy watching the blood drain from that pretty face."

I clenched my hands, readying myself for impact and my fingers caught on the tail of the chain wrapped around my neck. I wound it around my hand, leaving some of the tail loose. The guard cocked his gun, and I swallowed down the bile that rose into my throat. Before he pulled the trigger, I whipped the tail of the chain hard and fast at his hand, lashing his skin and causing the gun to fly out of his grip. He cried out as he stumbled back, clutching his wounded hand.

Suddenly, Zayn hurdled into him, knocking him to the ground. Before the guard could plead for his life, Zayn shot two bullets into his head, leaving him wide-eyed and dead, with the look of fear frozen on his face.

A bomb went off on the far end of the courtyard, incinerating everything in proximity.

"Amelia!"

I looked over to Shyam, who was only a few feet away. He had managed to overtake Tarun, his powerful legs straddling the enemy, holding him in place. The gun had been knocked to the side, lying nearby.

"Run!" he shouted at me.

135

Tarun's cackling interrupted me before I could respond. "Shyam Sethi. Always the cocky one. You always think you have the upper hand. Always in control of the situation."

"Shut up, asshole. You don't get to have fun anymore with your stupid riddles." Shyam spat at his nemesis.

He looked up at me again, his eyes crazed with rage. "Amelia, dammit. Get. The. Fuck. Out."

Tarun's voice carried over the sounds of battle. "Even your girlfriend will not listen to you anymore. Because you're null. Unimportant. Irrelevant. You're just the snake who'll eventually get his head slit off. You'll never learn."

Shyam stared at him, bewildered by his words.

I saw Tarun's wrist shift under the weight of Shyam's body. A glint of silver shone between their bodies. It was too thin to be from a gun.

"Goodbye, old friend." Tarun pulled his wrist back, exposing what he was holding—a silver dagger. Shiny and sharp.

"Shyam! He has a dagger!" I screamed.

Shyam looked down to see the blade pointed to his abdomen. He rolled quickly to get off Tarun, but not quickly enough. The dagger pierced the side of his torso as he moved away.

As Shyam rolled to a stop, grabbing his side, Tarun dashed for the gun and aimed it at him. Shyam froze, staring down the barrel.

Thinking quickly, I ran over to Salena's body, struggling from the weight of the thick chain around my neck, and snatched up the gun that she had used. With a clear view of Tarun's back, I did my best to steady my shaking hand, aiming it at the monster who had terrorized us for far too long. I cocked the gun, gaining Tarun's attention as he turned his head in the direction of the sound. I could see the look of surprise mixed with anxiety on Shyam's face as he lay on his back, his eyes trained on me.

Tarun's eyes flashed with amusement when he realized it was me who held him at gunpoint. He started toward me; the dagger coated in Shyam's blood still in his hand. If I had learned anything from the beautiful woman lying dead in her own cold blood, it was to never hesitate. *Don't miss.* I pulled the trigger, releasing the final bullet of the war.

Tarun fell backward, blood spilling from his forehead. Shyam crouched over him, one hand on his wounded torso and the other holding Tarun's own dagger. "Goodbye. *Friend.*" In one swift move, he slit Tarun's throat to finish him off.

He discarded the weapon and stood up shakily, visibly uncomfortable from the wound in his side. Leaving Tarun to bleed out on the ground, he set his sight on me.

A look of relief and happiness washed over his face, erasing all the tension that had scarred him for years. He closed the distance between us slowly.

137

I dropped my hand with the still warm gun, then activated the safety and tossed it aside. I was ready to feel his embrace and absorb his kisses. I was ready to be surrounded by the safety of his arms, and I never wanted to leave it again.

"*Jaan?*" He stopped short of arms' length, concern washing over his face. "Are you okay? You're pale."

Just then, my legs gave out and I felt the hard impact of my knees on the ground. My vision blurred and my thoughts went fuzzy.

"AMELIA!" The last thing I heard was Shyam's cries before everything went black.

CHAPTER XIX

AMELIA

I was floating between clouds, my body light like the sheer white slip draped over my body. I finally felt free of the worries and obligations that had weighed me down for weeks.

My fingers grazed the subtle coolness of the clouds. Delicate silver raindrops tickled my skin as they fell, purifying all that had stained me in my other life.

As I rose higher, the raindrops grew larger and pelted my body with more force. Wind pushed and pulled my body angrily. I wanted it to stop. I didn't want to go any further.

The wind thrashed tendrils of my hair into my face and they lashed my skin violently. I squinted hard through the rain to see ahead of me, but all I could make out was a dark shadow. My body was pulled closer to the shadow. The figure came into focus, more monster than man.

Large hands reached out to grab me. I forced air through my windpipe to scream, but no sound came out. My limbs wouldn't work. I squeezed my eyes shut to block out the horrid figure. I was paralyzed as the hands grabbed me and a deep male voice shouted my name.

"Amelia!"

I opened my eyes, blinking desperately to get my surroundings in focus. Something was holding my shoulders down. Anxiety forced my breaths to grow short and uneven.

"Breathe," the deep voice soothed. I closed my eyes and focused on my breath, allowing air to fill my lungs and slowly exhaling it out.

"That's it, *jaan*." Memory of who that voice belonged to hit me like a truck. The low bass centered me and brought me to awareness. I took another cleansing breath before opening my eyes. A prayer. A silent wish that it was really him.

Shyam. I could see him clearly. He had more facial hair than I remembered, but it was him. The same intense hazel eyes and strong features.

He smiled as recognition washed over me. I felt his fingers stroke my hair as I nearly lost myself in his gaze.

I could see another person in my periphery. I tried to turn my neck to see who it was, but pain shot through the base of my skull and radiated to the tops of my shoulders. I flinched from the ache.

"Don't try to move," Shyam said softly. "You're safe now, in my house in India."

India. It all came back to me. The reason I was here was because I was kidnapped by Tarun. *Tarun!* Oh God. Had he survived?

As if reading my thoughts, he continued, "Tarun is dead. You killed him."

I remembered the wedding. I flexed my fingers as if I could still feel the weight of the gun between them.

He took my hands in his. "You suffered a severe concussion when his guard hit your head. You've been unconscious ever since."

I tried to speak but my voice came out raspy. My lips were so chapped that they hurt to move.

"Easy. It'll be difficult to speak since you haven't used your voice for a while." He brought a glass of water close to me and helped me drink from the straw. The cool water numbed my throat on the way down.

I cleared my throat and tried again. "How long have I been out?"

"About four days."

Four days?!

"This is Dr. Khan," he said introducing the man next to him. "He's been tending to you. He wants to check you out now, since you're awake. Are you okay with that?"

I nodded hesitantly.

Shyam grabbed my hand and squeezed it gently. "I'm not leaving you. Not ever again."

The doctor moved around Shyam so that he was closer to me. "Are you able to see my fingers clearly?" he asked, holding two in front of my eyes, and moving them around to watch me track them.

"Yes."

"Are you able to tell me your first and last name and where you are from?"

"Amelia Becker from Seattle, Washington."

"Very good," he said.

He continued to check the rest of my body, including the gash on my cheek, which was sealed up with stitches and covered with bandages. He also inspected the bottom of my feet, which had been pretty scratched up from being shoeless most of the time in captivity. He removed the IV that had kept me hydrated during my unconscious state and sealed the puncture on my arm with a piece of gauze and medical tape.

"Your cheek seems to be healing nicely, too. I'll be back in three days to remove the stitches. Keep the area clean and dry in the meantime. Also, stay off your feet as much as possible to give the blisters a chance to heal. Shyam has been taking great care of you, so let him keep doing so."

I narrowed my eyes, puzzled by his admission.

"I guess you wouldn't know since you were out cold, but he's been by your side since you came home. Wouldn't leave you alone no matter how hard I tried to convince him to get some rest for himself," he said as he packed up his medical bag.

I stared at Shyam, who wore a tender expression as he looked back at me. That probably meant he was the one who cleaned the dirt that had accumulated on my skin since I had been taken. Imagining him giving me a sponge bath made me blush.

"Before I go, I need to check your wounds too," the doctor said, pointing to a chair across from the bed, signaling for Shyam to sit.

I had completely forgotten about what Tarun did to him—the bite and the dagger. Stress tensed my brows as images from that day replayed in my head. Shyam squeezed my hand again to reassure me that he was okay. He followed Dr. Khan's order and sat on the chair. The doctor inspected the wounds on his neck.

"These are healing well. You're lucky he didn't get you too deep. It probably just bled a lot since this area is highly vascularized. Have you been continuing your course of antibiotics?"

"Yes."

The doctor motioned for him to lift his shirt. "Let me see your waist."

Shyam lifted the hem, exposing a reddish-pink scar.

The doctor pressed around the scar, causing Shyam's face to tense in discomfort. Reflexively, I moved to push myself up to go over to him but stopped when dizziness took hold of me and forced me back down on my bed of pillows.

"Don't," Shyam warned. I heeded his orders and stayed put, fighting my need to hold his hand through his pain.

"Scar tissue is minimal. No damage to any organs. Continue massaging the area around the incision to promote proper healing and minimize scarring."

"I don't care about the scar, Doc," he said light-heartedly as he lowered his shirt.

The doctor gave Shyam a rundown of the antibiotics and pain medications I was to take for the next few days. To my embarrassment, Shyam asked him to leave me with birth-control pills so I could start them today and verified that they wouldn't interact with my course of antibiotics. The doctor obliged and bid us farewell, promising to return to remove my stitches in a few days.

The door clicked. After weeks of despair and loss, we were finally alone. Together.

Silence filled the space between us. Our eyes never broke contact.

I wished he would touch me just to ease the awkwardness I felt. I had longed for this moment in my dingy cell in Tarun's dungeon, and now that it was here and I was living it, I was too nervous. What should I say? What should I do? Maybe I should at least thank him for flying all this way to save me?

I cleared the bubble in my throat. "Um…thank you."

"For what?" he asked.

"Um…coming all the way from New York…to save me. I didn't think I'd get out of there."

"You did that all on your own. I didn't save you. You did it yourself."

Images of Salena lying lifeless in her wedding gown, surrounded by her own blood, replayed like scenes from a movie in my head. I hadn't kept my promise to her, to save her. I fought back the tears threatening to fall as I remembered how she looked splayed out on the ground in her wedding outfit.

"Hey. Talk to me." Shyam moved to lie next to me on the bed, wrapping his arms around me. I rested my head on his chest and let his steady heartbeat soothe my emotions.

"I couldn't save her," I whispered into his chest. My tears began to flow freely.

"You tried," he said as he rested his chin on my head. "This world isn't so kind to women. They pay the price for the decisions that we men make." He rubbed small circles on my back to comfort me.

"It's not fair. She didn't deserve this kind of life," I sobbed.

He was quiet. I felt as if he wanted to say something but was holding his words back.

"What happened to her afterward?" I had no recollection of anything after passing out soon after killing Tarun.

"Her father was waiting in the house to escort her to the ceremony and give her away when everything happened. He ran away from the house as soon as he heard the explosions. He always was a coward."

"So, he just left without his daughter?"

"Are you surprised? He forced her into two engagements, one of which she was held as a prisoner. He didn't even come back to give her a proper funeral because he was too scared of me. Jai and I took care of her funeral rites."

I couldn't imagine not attending your own daughter's funeral. She hadn't deserved him as a father. My heart was broken for her, yet thankful that in some way she was now resting in peace. "Tarun raped her. She didn't go into details, but I knew he used her when she'd disappear from her cell."

His body stiffened under me. I was sure hearing about his ex- endure that kind of torture wasn't easy, but there was something more. I pulled back from him to see his face. He was pale and looked like he was about to be sick.

"What is it?"

His jaw clenched and his lips were pressed tightly together, as if carefully considering his reply.

"Amelia. I need to know—Tarun said something back at his house."

I thought hard, trying to figure out what he was talking about. I remembered most everything that had happened, but the details were still fuzzy to me.

The softness that had been on his face this whole time disappeared. He looked at me like he was dreading what he was about to ask. "Did he...touch you?"

"What?" I asked in surprise.

"I need to know. It doesn't change how I feel about you, but I just need to know for peace of mind."

Desperate to keep his mind from wandering further down this vile path, I spoke quickly to settle him. "No. Not in that way."

He sighed out a big breath of relief. I felt his body relax again against mine.

147

I summoned what little courage I had left in me and back-tracked to what he had just said. "How *do* you feel about me?"

The intensity in his eyes burned brighter than I had ever seen. "*Jaan.* I thought you died. Tarun led me to believe that he killed you, and *that* killed me. I was a stubborn ass before and couldn't see clearly. I had to lose you to realize what an idiot I was for pushing you away. It should be pretty evident to you from my actions how I feel."

My heart hammered in my chest. He was saying all the things I had dreamt of him saying before being kidnapped. Back then, I would have given anything to hear him profess these feelings for me. Now, he *was* saying them, and I just stared back at him in disbelief.

He pulled out something silver from his pocket. It was the snake necklace that he had given me for my birthday. The same necklace that he gave me when he told me I was his partner. I had thought it was lost forever when Tarun took it from me.

"Where did you get that?" I whispered in shock.

"Tarun sent it to me after he kidnapped you. I thought you were dead when I received this."

He fastened the clasp around my neck. I looked down at the glittering pendant shining against my skin.

His hands held my neck. I was sure he could feel my pulse racing through my skin. "Amelia Becker. I love you."

I stopped breathing. I stopped thinking. Everything just stopped.

"I love you, too," I said through my tears.

He moved in without wasting another moment, pressing his lips to mine. His kiss was soft. This was my home, and I never wanted to leave again.

Our lips moved together saying everything else that we wanted to say to each other, but couldn't wait any longer to say. I tasted his masculine flavor mixed with my salty tears. Our tongues welcomed each other again as lovers, exploring territory that had been neglected for too long.

Shyam pulled away first, causing me to groan in protest.

"Did I hurt you?" he asked, touching the bandages on my cheek.

"Not at all." I smiled to reassure him of my honesty. "Maybe just a little bit with this," I said, pulling on his short beard.

He chuckled. "Not a fan of facial hair?"

"Not usually. But on you, it's sexy."

"Don't worry, it's going away."

"Why?"

"I refused to shave when I thought you died, then I sort of promised myself not to do it until I found you," he replied.

I laughed. "That's an interesting promise to make to yourself."

He chuckled. "I was a little too preoccupied to care about my looks."

"You still look like heaven, though," I teased, winking playfully.

He kissed my forehead. "You need your rest, *jaan*."

I felt a little tired, but I wasn't ready for him to leave me alone just yet. "Will you stay with me?"

He kicked off his shoes and undid the buttons on his shirt. Laying back against the pillows so I could tuck into his side, he said, "I was planning on it."

CHAPTER XX

SHYAM

Reorganizing the business after Tarun died was giving me a chronic headache. He was our major competitor, so with him gone, it meant that we now ruled the empire.

After Amelia killed him, Zayn retrieved Salena's body while I carried Amelia out of the venue. Jai detonated the rest of the explosives and narrowly escaped with the rest of our men, leaving Tarun's palace in ruins. Most of his men were killed, and those who weren't were executed. We couldn't risk any of his men with inside knowledge being free to associate with the rest of the drug network while we rebuilt our business.

The takeover of Tarun's clients was successful. Distributors didn't have much of a choice as to where their supply came from anymore. Clients were more than eager to bend over backward to be in my good graces again. In the drug trade, clients were rarely unconditionally loyal. Loyalty could be bought using enough money and an ounce of deceit. I would do business with them but would never forget how easily they had defected. Though, just the news of Jai and I taking down Tarun was enough to scare the shit out of the underworld. I didn't anticipate having another issue anytime soon.

Whenever Amelia was sleeping after taking her pain medication, I spent most of my time holed up in my office with Jai, going over accounts and making calls to coordinate shipments. Since Jai was a tech genius, it was easy to run our business from India instead of New York. We were able to access all the files that we needed and teleconference with our men who were running our factories in the States. Jai had to set up new accounts on our server for the new clients we had attained from Tarun.

Zayn also helped in the field to convert all Tarun's factories to become manufacturers for our products. It was a massive endeavor, but I couldn't be happier having the Sethi name as the major producer of product in the world. The dynasty finally belonged to us, and it was time to clean up shop.

Behind my desk, Jai was busy on his laptop, manually adding new accounts. It was a tedious job, but we didn't have access to Tarun's software to import any of the information we needed.

Meanwhile, I was busy reading through files on new clients. I had my men run extensive background checks on clients who were strictly from Tarun's original network—the network his father had intended for him to run without encroaching on mine. I was combing through the files to familiarize myself with the bullshit Tarun was involved in with them and memorize anything I could use to bribe them in the future if needed.

Jai stood up from his chair and stretched his arms overhead. He walked to the bar and busied himself with a drink before offering me a glass of scotch of my own.

"Thanks." I took a sip, thankful for something to wet my throat. I placed the glass down on the coffee table and returned to my reading.

Jai took a seat across from me. "You have a farmer's tan on your face," he said, pointing his glass toward my freshly shaven cheeks.

I smoothed my hand over my jaw. The Indian sun had tanned my skin except where it had been covered by my beard. My skin tone would even out in a matter of days with how strong the sun was. "Shut up. I still look better than you."

He chuckled. "What does Amelia think of it?"

"She prefers me without the facial hair," I said, thumbing through another file.

"How is she doing?" he asked.

I leaned back into my chair, taking my glass with me. "She's better. Still has her stitches in but the wound seems to be healing without much scarring."

"That's good to hear," he said, swirling the liquid in his drink. "Not going to lie, that thing turned my stomach when Tarun ripped her bandage off. I'm glad she was the one who got to kill him. She deserved revenge after the shit he did to her."

I wasn't too thrilled that I had introduced the woman I loved to a world of killing and criminals. Even though she said he never raped her, I still felt rage whenever I thought about the things she'd endured at his hand. Every time I looked at her cuts and bruises, I saw red. If she hadn't met me, she wouldn't have had to shoot anyone. She'd still be safe in her apartment in New York. "I wish it were one of us. Not her."

Jai nodded, understanding my reasons without an explanation. "I'm sorry I haven't been up to see her. I wanted to give you all space."

"I appreciate it. Even though she's recovering well, she still gets tired often and needs pain meds to be comfortable." When I wasn't in the office, I was taking care of her. I barely let Raj or any of the maids look after her. I preferred to personally change her dressings, feed her, and give her medication myself. I even bathed her every day, so she didn't need to stand on her feet for too long in the shower. She thought I was overdoing it, but I needed to do it. I felt guilty for not keeping her safe in the first place.

"When's her next check-up with the doctor?" he asked.

"Tomorrow."

He was quiet for a moment, as if considering his next words. "I'm proud of you."

I raised my eyebrow, unsure of what had prompted his praise.

"You dropped the selfish-prick shit and manned up."

I chuckled. "You're one to talk. You're the most selfish prick around."

"I'm still a bachelor, so I'm allowed to be one. When I find the right woman, I'll need to drop it too. But until then, I'll *prick* as much as I want." He flashed a sly grin before taking a sip of his drink.

"I told her I love her," I blurted it out.

His jaw dropped in disbelief. "No shit. How did you manage that one?"

"It just came out. I was stupid for pushing her away before."

He moved to the edge of his seat and leaned in toward me. "Do you want to marry her?"

I frowned. "It's a little too early to think about marriage, don't you think?"

"Is it? I mean, you both endured more than the average couple ever does in a lifetime."

"I guess you're right." I had been against marriage, but now, my mind was opening to so many things that I had never considered before. It wasn't off the table. Picturing Amelia as my wife and pregnant with my child tugged at my heart in a way that I had never felt. But I didn't want to rush things yet. I had just gotten her back and wanted to enjoy being together again.

Jai's expression turned serious. "Are you sure you want to keep her in this life, though?"

"Hold on. You're the one who kept harassing me to admit my feelings for her and prove my love to her, and now, when I tell you that I did it, you're questioning my decision?" I was so confused with his flip-flopping.

"Don't get me wrong. I love that you guys are finally together and in a relationship. I think she's perfect for your cold-ass heart. But you saw what this life did to Mom and Salena."

I had, and it was the reason I had been against marriage in the first place. "Tarun is gone, though."

"Yeah, but there'll be a new Tarun one day. We have too many enemies to never go through this again."

He was right. I thought about my conversation with Amelia when she lamented about how Salena had never deserved any of this. Amelia didn't deserve it either. "So, what do I do? Let her go?" The thought made me sick to my stomach. I thought she was gone for good once and that had killed me. I couldn't do it again.

"I don't know, man. But if you're going to marry her, then you need to really think long and hard about the impact *this* is going to have on her life and your kids' lives," he said, picking up one of the files from the table and waving it at me.

I was supposed to be relieved and happy that she was back with me, but instead I felt guilt gnaw at me. I didn't want to think about this anymore. "Breaktime over. Get back to work."

With that, I did what I had always done best—shut off my emotions.

CHAPTER XXI

AMELIA

"Hold still. This part will feel strange."

I shut my eyes tightly to keep from seeing the scissors Dr. Khan was using to remove my stitches.

I could barely feel anything, but I still felt queasy just thinking about someone cutting strings out of my cheek.

"Done," announced Dr. Khan, before he backed away to pack his instruments into his bag.

Shyam looked at me expectantly. He had barely left my side since he brought me to the house. He argued with his staff when they tried to wait on me. I had asked his butler, Raj, if I could eat dinner downstairs one evening and Shyam nearly had a heart attack when he saw me trying to walk down the stairs to the dining room. I insisted I was fine and that he was being paranoid. Instead, he shoo-ed me back into my room after screaming at the poor man. He made Raj bring up our meals and ate with me in bed. I loved having Shyam to myself, but I wasn't an invalid. I had been held captive once before, and I didn't want to be again, even if this time my captor was smoking hot.

I opened my mouth, stretching my jaw around in circles to feel for anything strange. "Feels normal."

The doctor held up a mirror for me. I could barely see anything except for a faint pink line where I had been wounded. I grinned. "You're amazing, doctor! My skin looks completely normal."

Dr. Khan smiled. "Use this salve twice a day on the scar," he said, handing me a small jar of ointment. "It'll help minimize its appearance some more. Also, be sure to wear sunscreen when you go out into the sun to help the scar disappear."

"Will do," I replied, handing the mirror back.

"Your vital signs all seem normal and your body seems stronger than when I first saw you, so you don't need bed rest anymore. Just be sure to honor your body if you do feel tired and rest. But you're free to resume normal activity."

That was the best news I had heard all day. I smirked at Shyam, hoping he had the same dirty thoughts I did. Shyam had been too afraid to touch me in bed. The chemistry was still there, probably even stronger than before. Our gentle, loving kisses would turn hot and intense quickly, but Shyam would always stop it before it turned into anything more. He treated me like a porcelain doll, afraid I'd break from his touch. It was driving me insane. I hadn't had him inside of me for far too long and I mourned the loss. I thought about touching myself to relieve some of the edge, but then decided it was stupid to get off on my own when I had a perfectly functioning stud sleeping next to me. I just needed to convince him I wasn't going to shatter to pieces if he touched me. On second thought, I was quite sure I *would* shatter in all the right ways if he did.

"Thank you, Dr. Khan." I shook his hand and then Shyam walked him out of the house.

The bedroom I had been camping out in was more like a small apartment. The suite had a living area and lavish spa-style bathroom. The four-poster bed that I spent most of my time in was more than comfortable.

It wasn't Shyam's bedroom, but he slept next to me here every night. He would bring clothes into the room to dress after showering in the morning. I had yet to see his room, since he didn't allow me to wander through the house.

Large princess windows allowed for plenty of sunlight to shine into the room. Even though the house was fully air-conditioned, I could still feel the heat of the sun through the glass. I opted for lightweight, loose dresses from the clothing that the maids had stocked the closet with.

I was lying back on the bed in a light-blue, gauzy dress when someone knocked at the door. Only the maids or Raj ever knocked, so I assumed it was one of them.

"Come in."

Jai poked his head inside. "Hey, doll. Up for a visit?"

I sat up, eager for company. "Took you long enough to visit!"

He came over to the bed and kissed my cheek. "I wanted to give you some space. Shyam said you were getting your stitches out today, so I thought I'd come check on you."

I leaned back against the headboard. "I'm great."

Taking a seat at the foot of the bed, he inspected my cheek. "Looks good. Doc did a good job."

"So, what have you been up to?" The last time I had seen him was at the wedding, so I hadn't had a chance to talk to him in a long time.

"Salvaging the business," he said.

Jai looked just as tired as Shyam did. I knew Shyam had been working day and night to take care of me and repair the business. He looked tired from taking care of everything and everyone. Hopefully, since Dr. Khan said I was okay to carry on as before, he could focus more of his energy on work. "That big of a mess?"

"You have no idea," he replied as he let out a big exhale. "Tarun was involved in some deep shit."

I laughed. "And drug dealers like you and Shyam aren't involved in deep shit?"

He nodded, a hint of seriousness washing over his usual carefree expression. "He made our business look like child's play. We basically sell candy compared to the stuff he did."

I believed it. Tarun was crazy and I was scared to think of the sick things he was involved with, so I didn't ask for details.

"So, how much longer are you planning to stay in India?" I asked, trying to change the topic.

"Maybe a couple weeks, until we straighten out some of this mess. I'll head back to New York to take care of Sethi Tech until Shyam gets back."

Shyam and I hadn't discussed what would happen next. It made sense that we'd return to New York eventually, but now that my job was over at Sethi Tech there would be no need for me to continue working there. I had negotiated a letter recommendation for my work so I could use it at my next job to further my career, but truthfully, I didn't want to leave Sethi Tech or Shyam. I didn't know what would happen next in our relationship. He said he loved me, but we hadn't discussed the future yet. Had his views on marriage changed? Did he want to marry me? Did he even want children? Uncertainty was swimming in my head.

"You okay there?" Jai's voice interrupted my thoughts. "If I didn't know better, I'd think that you wanted to stay here forever or something," he teased.

I shrugged my shoulders, trying to avoid seeming too desperate to keep things the way they were. "I miss New York, but India isn't so bad."

"Really?" he asked. "You haven't even experienced it yet and you like it?"

I liked the intimacy that I had with Shyam here. I didn't like thinking about the unknown that would greet us when we returned to New York. "I mean, I get to lounge around all day in this huge palace and the people who work here are nice. So far, not much to complain about."

Jai saw through my words. "I take it you all haven't discussed the future yet?"

"How did you know?" I asked.

"I talked to Shyam and he seemed quick to brush the subject off."

That was news to me. Avoiding talk of our future wasn't a good sign. "I see."

"It's not like before," he said, trying to keep me from spiraling into the web of anxiety that I was creating in my brain. "He doesn't seem like he's afraid to commit to you. He just feels guilty."

I was unsure why Shyam would feel that way. "Why?"

He let out a deep sigh. "He really should be having this conversation with you, but I'll give you the short version. He blames himself for your kidnap and subsequently getting hurt."

Why did that surprise me? I should have known he'd feel that way. He had felt so broken that his mother died because of his father's career. He probably felt like he was just repeating history and that I could easily meet the same fate as his mother. "That's ridiculous."

"Is it? If you didn't know us in the first place, you wouldn't be halfway around the world right now."

"You have a point," I replied. But things happened for a reason. If I hadn't met them, I wouldn't have met the love of my life. It was a fucked-up story but was *our* story.

"I love you all together," he said, putting his hand on my knee to comfort me before continuing. "You're good for my brother. But our world is dangerous, and this won't be the last time that someone tries to target the people that Shyam loves."

I felt helpless in this situation. "Am I just supposed to move back to New York and move on without him? Because I can't do that."

"I don't know what you're *supposed* to do. But I just think you should consider your safety when thinking about the future. Would you really be able to live a life looking over your shoulder? Waiting for the next bad guy to take you or even your children and use you as ransom?"

My stomach churned thinking of anyone touching my children.

He squeezed my knee. "I'd love for you to join our family and be my sister more than anything. But as your *brother*, I fucking love you too, and I don't want anything to happen to you again."

I smiled. We really did feel like family. "You're a fucking softy, you know that?"

He chuckled. "I won't kick your ass for saying that unless you tell anyone else. Can't let the ladies know I'm soft inside."

I threw my pillow at him and laughed loudly when it smashed into his face.

"Why are you two always giggling when I walk in on you together?" Shyam had returned, and judging from his expression, he was less than amused at our pillow fight.

Jai threw the pillow at Shyam, hitting him harder than my poor excuse of an attack. "Because we think the way you look is hilarious," Jai joked.

Shyam rolled his eyes as he set the pillow back on the bed.

Redirecting his attention to me, Jai said, "So, since you're all better, we should go out for a celebratory dinner."

That was a wonderful idea. I was excited to finally break out of this bedroom and join the real world again. I wanted to explore the country and try all the food that I had heard about over the years. However, before I could fervently accept his invitation, Shyam interrupted, "No. Absolutely not. She still needs to rest."

Jai argued on my behalf. "Oh, come on! She's been locked up in a cell for weeks and now you're going to just lock her up in a room all day?"

Shyam gave his brother the death stare. "Shut up. She's been through a lot and she needs to recover properly."

"How about asking *her* what she wants?" I interjected. I stood up and put my hands on my hips, waiting for him to realize how stubborn he was being.

"We'll discuss this later," he dismissed me, trying to end the conversation on his terms.

"No. We'll discuss it now," I shouted.

Jai snickered and leaned back onto the bed on his side, propping his head up with his hand. He was enjoying the show.

Shyam glared at his brother before addressing me. "*Jaan.* You need your rest. When you build back your strength, we can discuss going out."

I glared at him. "Are you fucking kidding me?"

Shyam growled at my persistence. Jai mouthed, "Oh shit," into the air and shuffled to sit upright to get a better view.

"Watch it," Shyam barked at me.

"You *watch it*. I know better than you what I've been through, and I want to go out."

"Come on, *bhaiya*. Please, can we go out?!" Jai chimed in, his voice dripping with sarcasm.

"Get the fuck out," Shyam yelled at him.

"Don't yell at him!" I screamed, rising on tiptoes to match his naturally intimidating stature.

Shyam's eyes widened in disbelief at how I had spoken to him.

"I'm out," Jai surrendered. "You all need to either beat each other up or fuck this out. Either way, I'll leave you to it. Let me know when you decide on dinner," he said before closing the door, leaving us alone.

Shyam and I stood still, facing off. No one wanted to be the first to give in. I was the one who had been kidnapped and locked away. Despite any guilt he felt over his role in my kidnapping, I was the only one who could know when I was ready to rejoin the world, and I wasn't going to let him win.

He moved in closer, shadowing me in his presence. The air between us was charged. He was so close I could feel his warm breath on my skin. Goosebumps spread over my neck and chest. If he got any closer, he would be pressed against me.

A low rumble from his throat was my only warning that he was about to attack. Hands grabbed me, holding me tight against his hard body. His lips moved in to devour me. Our kiss was a blur of lips, tongues, and teeth as we licked, sucked, and bit like feral animals in heat.

His lips moved to that special part of my neck that he knew would drive me wild. His big, firm hands slid down my body and under the hem of my dress. He palmed my ass cheeks, pushing my pelvis flush against him in rhythmic strokes. I needed him. Now.

My fingers worked quickly, pulling his t-shirt over his head, and then working the fly of his jeans and pushing them down and off his legs. I pulled my dress over my head and threw it across the room. He chuckled at my haste.

I stood before him in my matching black satin bra and panties that I had found in my drawer this morning. All the underwear provided for me were made of the highest-quality fabrics I had ever seen. Everything was made of fine satin or lace. I would have bet Shyam had a say in what was provided to me.

Hungry eyes roamed my thin frame. I had lost weight while in captivity and hadn't gained it back yet, and I was self-conscious of how I looked. If he noticed my nervousness, he didn't let on that he was aware of it. "You're beautiful."

I pulled him down to kiss me, my arms clinging around his neck. I backed us up onto the bed, his massive body encasing me against the mattress. His tongue worked down my neck and between my breasts. The ache under my panties was too painful to ignore any longer. I wrapped my legs around his hips, pulling his cock closer to me. I rubbed myself against him, with only our underwear in the way. "I need you, babe."

He pressed a gentle kiss to my lips. "We shouldn't. You should be taking it easy." He tried to move off me, but I held him firmly in place with my thighs.

"Stop treating me like glass. I'm not going to break."

He exhaled a heavy breath. "You don't know what it was like for me when I thought you were dead." His gaze fell to the mattress as if to avoid mine. He didn't want to show me the sorrow that filled his eyes.

I lifted his chin up, so I could stare deeply into his eyes. "But I'm not and I want to *live*. I don't want to be locked in a tower anymore. I'm finally free and I want to experience everything I've missed out on."

He sighed. "I don't want to hurt you."

"I'll be okay. I promise," I whispered.

He studied me as if weighing his options in his head. "Tell me to stop the minute it's too much for you."

I smiled, looking at this dear man who put my safety before his needs. How did I get so lucky? "I love you."

He returned the adoration that I felt for him in my heart. "I love you, too," he said, rubbing the tip of his nose against mine.

He continued tasting me everywhere, from my mouth down to my bellybutton, sending chills through my body. His fingers hooked my panties and pulled them off my legs, the journey lasting longer than I could bear.

As he nestled between my legs, my desperate flesh was on full display for him. His hands held my legs in place as he moved in on me, his tongue meeting my wet pussy. My back arched off the bed from a single stroke. I couldn't hold back the loud moan that came from deep within my core. It had been so long since I had been touched there and I was so sensitive.

He continued his assault on my clit. Each swipe of his tongue was more painful than the last. The pressure waiting to be released was too much. "Shyam. Please. I need you in me."

"*Jaan*, I'm rock fucking hard. If I fuck you now, I'll tear you in half. I need you ready for me first."

God, his words drove me wild. His desire for me was like a vibrator humming on that perfect spot that guaranteed release.

His tongue worked me over as he slipped two fingers inside of me. I knew I was sopping wet from how easily they slid inside. His fingers fucked me good, hitting the right spot at the top of my inner wall each time they entered. I couldn't hold back any longer. I exploded around his fingers, gripping them tight with the force of my orgasm. I saw God, stars, and the whole fucking universe as I cried out.

I gasped for breath as I came down from my high. Shyam rose from between my legs and covered my body with his. "I missed that sound," he whispered in my ear.

I gave him a lazy smile, still in my haze of bliss.

He pushed his boxers down, freeing his massive erection. I hadn't thought I could forget how big he was, but apparently, I had. My eyes widened at his size. Would he still fit inside of me? I hadn't had sex in a long time, and I was surely too tight to fit all of him in me. I chose not to think about it anymore and kissed him hard, losing my thoughts as we breathed into each other.

His hands pushed the cups of my bra down. He moved his mouth over one nipple, sucking and biting it, causing me to squirm from sensation. Then he showered attention onto my other side. He treated each one like it was his favorite.

I placed my hands on his rigid chest, pushing him up slightly so his eyes could meet mine. I was ready. He read my thoughts. "Are you sure?"

I nodded. He reached into the drawer of the nightstand beside the bed and pulled out a condom. I had only been on birth control for a few days, so were supposed to use protection until the hormone levels were effective. He lined up his protected dick with my slit. I closed my eyes and took a deep breath, waiting for him. "Look at me," he gently ordered me.

I stared into his eyes, losing myself in his magnetism. I felt his tip slide in smoothly. It didn't feel as tight as I thought it would, so I relaxed a little more, and he pushed farther. I cried out from the pain—I had spoken too soon. I was too tight, and he was too big.

He moved his hand between us. Two fingers formed a V so that the length of both stroked the sides of my slit to help loosen me up for him. The split between his knuckles massaged my clit, giving me friction to rub against. Inch by inch, he pushed farther until he was fully inside, groaning from how tight I squeezed him. I felt so full. He must have felt it too because he paused to let his dick rest inside of me and stretch my walls.

Flames ignited in his eyes. He pressed both hands into the mattress alongside my head and began his punishment. His strokes were long and complete, touching the far reaches of my pussy. His pace quickened and I could tell he couldn't stop even if I begged him to. He was a man possessed. This was water for his thirst, food for his hunger, and prayer for his soul.

I panted along with him. I could feel myself reaching my threshold again. We raced to the finish line together with each slam against each other. I screamed as I fell over the edge, my vision going black since the only thing my body could do was feel. I felt the sweat on his pelvis against my skin. I felt his length thicken inside of me, ready to burst. I felt his ferocious growl as he found his release and collapsed onto me.

I held him to me, my hand cupping the back of his head as our heartbeats steadied to baseline together.

When we caught our breaths and we could form sentences with our words, he rolled to the side of me. His body turned to face mine. The backs of his fingers stroked my cheek. "Are you okay?"

"I'm great." I was stupidly happy and couldn't stop smiling. "I love you."

"I love you so fucking much."

We stayed just like that, gazing into each other's eyes and stroking each other until sleep overtook us.

CHAPTER XXII

AMELIA

Waiting for her to answer the phone that Shyam had given me was the most nerve-wracking thing ever.

RING. RING. RING.

It was late in Seattle with the time difference. Maybe she was asleep. I wished it would just go to voicemail, but I'd have to have this conversation eventually.

"Hi, dear! Long time, no hear."

The love in her voice killed me. I was about to lie to her, and I hated myself for it. I found a bench across from one of the many ornate fountains in the courtyard and took a seat, needing to sit down for this conversation.

"Hey, Mom. How's it going?"

"I should be asking you the same. No call for weeks? I was so worried about you."

"I'm so sorry, Mom. I'm a horrible person." At least that part was the truth.

"I called your friend Natalie and she said that you were on a work trip. Is that true?"

When I was kidnapped, Jai called Natalie to explain that I had been called away on an impromptu work trip for the company. Shyam knew that my mom and friends would start to worry and try to get the police involved. He hadn't been sure he wanted to tell my mother anything until he knew for certain I wouldn't be coming back.

I had texted Nat earlier and she was pissed at me for not personally telling her about the "work trip," too. I got her to forgive me by promising to hook her up with any eligible bachelors I found here.

"Yes. I'm sorry I didn't get a chance to tell you, but it was very—uh—sudden." *I'm so going to hell.*

"Amelia. That's unacceptable." *Here it comes.* "You should have called me as soon as you reached there."

"I know. There just wasn't much time after I arrived, and work has been chaotic ever since." *Definitely going to hell. Like a ninth-circle-of-hell deal.*

176

"I understand that you have your own life and career now and you're not a child, but you're still *my* child and I deserve a heads-up. Maybe even a text until you get the chance to call."

"Mommy, I'm a crappy person." There was no point denying it. "I really feel terrible about waiting so long to call you."

She sighed on the other end. "Are you safe in India?"

"Yes. I'm living in—corporate housing right now." *Please don't ask for my address.*

"What kind of project are you working on? Nat said it was something confidential and that she didn't know details." Jeeze, those Sethi brothers were good liars. They had set this whole thing up to avoid as many potential questions as possible from people who knew me.

"Yeah, it involves really sensitive data that can't be shared," I lied.

"Hmm. That sounds exciting, dear. When do you return to New York?"

Shyam and I really needed to have a talk about where our relationship was going and what we were planning to do next. He had to return to New York eventually, since his headquarters was there, and I never imagined living in India for the rest of my life. "I'm not sure yet."

"Well, are you able to have visitors?" she asked.

Oh shit. "You want to visit—here?" *Noooooo.*

177

"I have some vacation days available and I've never been to India. I'd love to spend some time with my daughter in a new country!" Her excitement was killing me.

Thinking fast, I responded, "I need to ask my boss first and then I can let you know."

"Speaking of, how's the boss-boyfriend? I assume he's there too?" I could hear the smirk in her voice.

"Uh—yeah."

"Are you living together?" I had known that was coming.

"Nope. I'm alone at my company apartment. He has some big mansion of his own." It was better if she didn't know I was shacking up with him. She'd jump to marriage and baby talk if I confirmed it.

"Mmmmmhmmm." *Shit.* She wasn't buying it. "Honey, I just want you to be responsible. You're a grown woman, but just be smart and safe."

I appreciated that she was just looking out for me. "I know, Mom."

"How are things with him?" she asked.

I kicked off my shoes and lay back onto the seat of the bench, bending my knees so my feet could rest flat. Things had never been better between us. We said "I love you" and he treated me with a tenderness that I hadn't felt before. It was like I was walking on air. "Amazing."

"That's so great to hear. I want to meet him, maybe when I visit you?" *God, she was persistent.*

I smiled. "That would be great." I was excited that she approved of my relationship with Shyam so far, but I really needed to make sure she didn't come to visit.

"Sweetheart, I need to go to bed now. It's late here and I have work in the morning." Her voice sounded heavy with sleep.

"Of course, Mom. I love you."

"I love you so much, Amelia. Let's Facetime next time so I can see your beautiful face."

"Sounds great. Bye."

"Bye."

I shut my eyes tight and let out a huge exhale that I had been holding in for too long. That was difficult as hell, and I felt like shit for lying.

The sun was too hot, and I felt like I needed a nap from the heat in addition to the exhaustion from my conversation with my mother. I slid on my shoes and made my way into the house.

Just walking to and from the courtyard was tiring. The house was enormous and going from point A to point B almost always felt like a hike. Now I knew why Shyam had kept me sequestered in my room to rest.

The cool air inside the house instantly relieved me. I followed the long corridors adorned with colorful pieces of art and sculptures. The house was opulent, decorated in whites and creams with dark wood furniture. It was a stark contrast to Shyam's homes in New York, which were sleek and masculine with cool grey tones. This house looked like the type of home that wealthy families owned for generations.

My sandals slapped against the shiny marble floors as I walked. I had always thought shoes were not allowed in Indian homes, but I noticed that everyone in this house wore them inside. I asked Raj about that and he joked that "the boys were too modern."

He was a sweet man. I could tell that Shyam respected him from how he interacted with him. Even though Raj was employed by him, Shyam spoke to him with reverence. Raj looked after him as if Shyam were his son. It was a special relationship.

In the distance, I could hear the loud chatter of the staff as they worked in the kitchen. Laughter and conversation sounded over the clatter of pots and pans. I loved the energy of the people who worked here—so happy and cheerful.

The warm smell of fried dough and spices danced into my nostrils, making my stomach growl. I had just eaten a delicious lunch of some sort of flatbread and savory chickpeas with a side of a cooling yogurt with chopped cucumber. I was ready for more.

I made my way up the long, circular staircase to my room. I still hadn't seen the entire house yet, but I was betting that this place had at least ten bedrooms from how massive it was. Exhausted from the trek, I finally reached my door. I turned the knob, so ready to crawl in bed—

The room was bare. The sheets had been stripped off the bed and my medication and phone charger were missing from my nightstand. I ran to the bathroom and didn't see any of my toiletries. My closet was empty too. *What the hell?*

I was so confused. I ran out of the room in search of Shyam.

I found his office on the first floor. I knocked on the door.

His deep voice sounded. "Come in."

I peeked my head inside. "Are you busy?"

"I'm always busy, *jaan*." He was sitting behind his desk, in front of his laptop screen. His white shirt was unbuttoned to reveal a hint of his toned chest and his sleeves were rolled up to his elbows, showing off the thick veins of his forearms. He was sexy even while working from home.

I came inside and shut the door anyway. "I have a problem."

That got his attention. He pushed back his chair and focused on me. Concern was etched on his face. "What's wrong?"

"My stuff. It's all missing."

His eyebrows furrowed. "What do you mean?"

I approached his desk and stood on the side of it closest to him. "I went to my room and everything was gone."

He smirked at me like he thought I was crazy. "Your stuff is in *your* room."

"What? No. I'm telling you! It's all gone!" I raised my voice in frustration. Here I was, completely confused and he was writing off my concerns.

He stood up from his chair and took my hand in his. "Let's look again." He led me out of the office and back up to my room.

"I know what I saw. It's not there. I swear, I'm not crazy!" I tried to convince him.

"Never said you were." He kept walking, leading the way.

We made it up to my door, but he didn't stop there. He kept leading me further away.

Now I was even more bewildered. "Where are we going?"

At the end of the floor, we reached a set of huge French doors. He opened them to let me in, and I slowly stepped inside.

I stood in the middle of a large living room complete with cream and wood furniture and marble-top tables.

"Keep going." He motioned for me to venture ahead, through an arched entry way that led to another room.

I traveled with him in tow. A giant, welcoming bed stood in the middle of the room, with plush white sheets and pillows. The walls were painted white with panels of intricately carved wood around the room.

"Is this your room?" I asked in amazement.

"It's *ours*." He grinned at me with his hands in his pockets.

I saw my medication on one of the nightstands with my charger. He opened one of the drawers in the dresser, revealing my neatly folded underwear. My clothes were organized by color and type and hung in the massive walk-in closet. It was like I had been using this room as my bedroom the whole time.

"You did this?" I looked around, unable to hide my astonishment.

"Well, not *me*. The maids moved everything. But yes, it was my idea."

I didn't know what to say. "Thank you."

"Don't thank me. Where else would you stay, other than with me?"

I shrugged. "I don't know. I thought you'd want your space?"

He put his hands on my arms, holding me close to him. "I haven't left your bed since I got you back and you think I'm going to keep you in a separate room? I put you in the guestroom because it was the easiest to access by Dr. Khan and the staff. This is our room now."

I grinned stupidly. I was so in love with this man.

Without saying a word, I knelt in front of him on the floor. Now, he was the one who looked confused.

Ready to show him my appreciation, I unfastened his belt, giving him my most seductive smile.

His hooded eyes watched me as he awaited my next move. "If this is you thanking me, then keep going, *jaan.*"

I pulled down his slacks, taking his boxers along with them. His dick was erect and ready for my attention. But then again, when wasn't it ready?

He pushed the top of my dress down, exposing my hard nipples. His fingers weaved into the hair at the back of my head, holding on like his life depended on it.

My mouth watered in anticipation of his taste. I licked my lips, thirsty for his precum. Instead of using my hands to hold his strong shaft in place, I clasped them behind my back, intertwining my fingers. My back arched as a result, causing my breasts to jut out like they were a gift being presented to a king—my king. Desire shone in his eyes as he looked down at my offering.

I wrapped my lips around his head and gave it a gentle suck, tasting the smooth skin. He threw his head back, emitting from his throat a deep groan that travelled down his body, causing vibrations that shook his tip in my mouth.

Having a man this powerful submit to my mercy aroused me like nothing else. His pleasure motivated me to working him harder. With each suck, I increased my pressure and took more of his length into my mouth. My hands clasped tighter behind my back from the excitement. Every so often, his shaft would twitch and slide out of my mouth, causing his arousal to wet my lips and chin on the way out. He seemed to enjoy the lack of control from not using my hands, because he would grip my head tighter in response.

I made my way further down his shaft, devouring him like a popsicle on a hot day—the kind that made your mouth water and juice leak out the sides of your mouth. When I couldn't fit anymore of him inside of me, he came to my rescue, tipping my head back at an angle so he could push in until I reached his balls. My nostrils flared, drawing in breaths to help steady my gag reflex. Through watery eyes, I peered up at the intoxicating man who had me drunk on lust and love on my knees.

"Fucking hell. That mouth," he managed to say in between pants. He thickened inside of me, standing more rigid than before, like he was made of steel. I felt him close to his release and plotted my next move.

I pressed my tongue to the underside of his length as I sucked him quicker, milking him as he fucked my mouth. He grasped my head with both his hands and spilled his hot liquid down my throat. His cry echoed in my ears. I swallowed as much as I could in one go, but there was too much left after just one gulp. I emptied the reserve in my mouth and released him from the grasp of my lips with a *pop*.

Sitting back on my heals, I admired my work. Shyam's eyes glowed with amazement. "Where the fuck did you learn that?"

I smiled slyly. "I had some inspiration."

He extended his hand to help me off the floor. Pulling me close to him and wrapping his arms around my body, he said, "Your inspiration has inspired me. Undress and get on the bed."

I giggled playfully. "Happy to play a role in you 'paying it forward.'"

He backed me up to the bed. "I'll show you how *charitable* I can be."

"I wouldn't mind a demonstration," I said, slipping my dress down my body and discarding it onto the floor. I turned to climb onto *our* bed.

"Prepare yourself for the show of your life." He smacked my ass cheek hard before lowering his head between my legs.

CHAPTER XXIII

AMELIA

"Everyone's here," Shyam said.

"I just need five more minutes." I smiled apologetically, still fussing over my hair in the bathroom mirror.

"Okay. Meet us down there when you're ready." He gave me a kiss on my cheek before shutting the bedroom door.

Jai and I had successfully convinced him to have a dinner at the house with a few of his men. He had frowned against having more of them in attendance when I pressed him—something about them being "too lewd to attend a dinner party." I think it was more about him not trusting them around any woman he was dating because he was madly overprotective.

I compromised and asked if we could just have a small dinner with Saran, Javed, and Zayn to thank them for coming to rescue me. I hadn't seen Zayn since the day of the wedding, and I also wanted to apologize for breaking his trust when I left the car despite his warning.

I fluffed my hair up one last time and applied a coat of lip gloss to my lips. The scar on my face was completely unnoticeable now, and I had put on the few extra pounds I needed, which made my cheeks seem fuller. The pallor of my skin was no longer there, and I looked healthier. Healthy and happy. Definitely happy.

How could I possibly have been miserable after spending all night making love to the man that I loved? Things were amazing between us. There was an openness and honesty that had never been there before. We talked about everything over dinners and in the wee hours of the night between sex sessions. He told me of his childhood with Jai and stories about his parents. I shared stories about growing up in Seattle and my awkward adolescence.

The only thing we hadn't discussed yet was the future. Honestly, I was nervous to broach the topic. We had finally reached a great place and I didn't want to mess it up. He didn't react well to neediness, and I didn't want to come off as a naggy girlfriend.

I turned off the bathroom light and slipped on my shoes before heading out of the room.

The guys were all gathered in the sitting area adjacent to the dining room. Watching these strong, strapping men all sitting around with tumblers of liquor in hand did something to me. It was a sexy sight to witness. And knowing that the most powerful one of them all was all mine was enough to make my thighs squeeze together to ease the resulting pressure.

Shyam noticed me and came to my side. "*Jaan*. You look beautiful."

"Thanks." I blushed and tucked a lock of hair behind my ear.

The other men followed suit, rising from their seats. Jai approached me first and kissed my cheek. "Hey, neighbor."

"Long time, no see!" I joked. Jai lived in the same house but stayed in a private apartment of his own on the opposite end of the estate. I ran into him around the house when he was working with Shyam and sometimes had lunch with him. For the most part, he preferred the privacy of his own apartment to enjoy his bachelor life without disturbing his brother. I never saw any of the women he brought home, but I overheard the maids talk in broken English about how easy they were and how they constantly had to clean up underwear and condoms from his private pool. *Yuck*! I didn't want a visual of Jai in some sort of wild orgy, but the man could charm the pants off anyone.

189

Javed and Saran both greeted me with handshakes and commented on how well I looked. I thanked them for coming all this way to help me.

Zayn approached me and wrapped his arms around me in a big bear hug. His embrace was caring and full of emotion, like that of a sibling. "You look great."

I let go of him and stood back, grinning. "Thanks."

"Shyam taking good care of you?" he asked, resting a hand on my shoulder.

From my periphery, I eyed Shyam, who kept his eyes on me cautiously. I nudged his arm with my elbow. "Too good." He was jealous of any guy who touched me, even if they were practically his family.

"You're behaving yourself?" Zayn smirked.

I scrunched up my nose, embarrassed by the trouble I had caused everyone. "About that. I'm really sorry for not listening to you that day."

All four men stood silently staring at me as I spoke, making me feel even more on the spot. I wouldn't have blamed them for hating me for the shit I had put them through. My armpits were sweaty, but I continued with my apology.

"I was stupid and stubborn, and I really regret putting everyone at risk," I said as I looked around and addressed each of them.

Shyam wrapped an arm around my waist, offering a silent act of forgiveness.

"I was pretty pissed that you didn't listen to me, but it worked out in the end. The bastard is gone because of you, so maybe we should be thanking you." Zayn grinned, hands in his pockets.

"You're not angry?" I glanced around the circle of men around me.

Saran waved his hand in the air. "Water under the bridge."

"Really?" I asked in relief.

"If we got mad every time any one of us was too stubborn to follow a plan, we'd never get anything done," Jai said.

The guys laughed in agreement.

"*Jaan.* It worked out in the end," Shyam murmured near my ear, rubbing circles on my back with his hand.

"Let's eat. I'm fucking hungry," Jai announced as though that was that and made his way into the dining room.

Conversation flowed as easily as the drinks. One would think that so much testosterone and power in one room would stifle dinnertime chat, but not tonight. These men were tough but warm when they were not on guard. The conversation frequently roamed to inappropriate topics like hooking up with women and bashing other men's heads in, courtesy of Jai.

Zayn was the politest of the gang. He was the most muscular of the group, with muscles barely contained by his t-shirt, yet he seemed to be the gentlest. His smile was endearing. He was considerate of my presence at the table and redirected the conversation when he felt it became too vulgar.

Shyam was at the head of the table, with me to his left. He was relaxed and actually smiling for most of the evening. He held my hand on the table when we weren't eating and kept gazing over to see if I was enjoying myself. We locked eyes often and both found it hard to be the first to tear our gaze away.

I saw glimpses of us in the future as we sat together with friends—married and hosting dinner parties just like this in our home. Maybe our children would be upstairs while we entertained our guests, and we would sneak away to check on them as they slept soundly in their warm beds. Jesus, I had it bad for him!

My belly was stuffed from the delicious meal. Raj had made his famous *biriyani*—a rice dish with lamb marinated in spices and yogurt. The meat was so tender, and the rice was so flavorful. I ate two platefuls at Raj's encouragement to have more. Shyam was still on his staff to fatten me up after my kidnapping. For dessert, we had a dish made of sweet cream molded into little balls in a syrup that tasted like cloves and cardamom.

I lay back in my chair, unable to sit upright from the pressure in my stomach. "That was delicious! I'm so full."

"Raj does make the best biriyani," said Saran.

"Have you tried his *chaat* yet?" asked Zayn as he wiped the corners of his mouth with his napkin before placing it back on his lap.

I creased my brows. My experience with Indian food was limited to the dishes I'd had in restaurants back home and whatever the staff fed me. "What's *chaat*?"

Zayn stared at me in shock. "Street snacks. You know…like *samosas* and *pani puri*?"

"Oh yeah…*samosas*. I know about those." I loved those little triangular pastries stuffed with potatoes.

"Please tell me you've had it from a street cart?" Javed asked.

I stared blankly at him.

"Shyam. You haven't taken her out for street food?" Zayn interrogated him.

Jai laughed. "Shyam has her on a leash. She hasn't stepped out of this house since the day he brought her here."

The men all stared at me in shock. Then they turned their focus on their boss.

Shyam clenched his jaw. "Stop staring at me or I'll rearrange your faces."

"What's wrong with you, man? She's all this way from home. The least you could do is take her out to enjoy some good food and sightseeing."

I secretly loved everyone ganging up on Shyam. People were usually too scared to confront him, so this was entertaining to watch. I put my hand over my mouth to cover my smile.

"You're enjoying this, *jaan*?" he asked, seemingly irritated by the pressure.

I giggled. "A lot!"

"Don't deflect. Be a good host and take her out tomorrow," Jai said.

My eyes lit up. "Please! I'd love to go out and experience India!"

"See? The poor girl is deprived of human interaction. She spends all day locked up in here looking at you," Jai continued, shamelessly poking at his brother.

"I'll think about it," Shyam said tossing his napkin on the table, clearly done with the conversation.

"If you don't take her, I will. And you know we're going to have a way more exciting time than she'd have with your boring ass." Jai winked at me.

"More like get arrested," Saran joked.

"Nah, the cops won't touch me if they know what's good for 'em." Jai pushed back from the table and nodded at the men. "Let's take this party to my place."

With that, we all stood to say our goodbyes.

"Thanks for the dinner, guys," Zayn said patting Shyam on the back and kissing my cheek. "You take care of yourself and call me if this guy messes up."

I smiled, appreciative of his concern. "I don't think I'll need to, but good to have a backup plan." I smirked, glancing at Shyam. He was less than amused.

The rest of the guys kissed me goodbye and left with Jai to live out every single man's fantasy of girls and booze. I bet Jai already had women at the apartment waiting for his return. One day, he'd get bored of this life. Until then, I guess he might as well enjoy himself.

I turned to Shyam and wrapped my arms around his neck, soothing his ego after his friends had ganged up on him. "Oh, don't be so pissy. You know they just like to harass you."

He kept his hands in his pockets, not giving in to me. "You like when they bother me."

"Only sometimes. You're cute when you're ticked."

That got a smile out of him. He wrapped his arms around my waist. "And you're cute *all* of the time."

I stood up on my tiptoes to kiss his lips. "Come upstairs and I'll show you how cute I can be."

He lifted one eyebrow in interest. I knew I had his attention and walked away swaying my hips as seductively as I could. I could feel his eyes on me, watching me as I moved away from him.

A moment later, I heard quick footsteps follow behind me as I made my way up to the bedroom. I smiled to myself, satisfied with my power over him.

***

I woke up to Shyam standing in the doorway of the closet, pulling his shirt over his head. He was dressed and ready for the day.

I rubbed my eyes and stretched my arms overhead. The room was still dark, so I assumed it was early morning.

I let out a huge yawn. He had kept me up for most of the night, fucking me until I passed out from exhaustion. The man's stamina was something else. "Where are you going?" I asked.

"We're going out."

Huh? I sat up in bed, my face scrunched up in confusion. "Where?"

"To see Punjab," he said, inserting his wallet into his jeans pocket.

My lips fixed into the most wicked smile ever. I leaned back onto the pillows and crossed my arms over my chest. "Well, well. Shyam Sethi finally gives in to peer pressure. I should have the boys over for dinner more often."

He fastened the clasp of his watch around his wrist. "Do you want to go out or not?"

I did, and I was scared if I pushed him far enough, he'd change his mind. *Mr. Grumpy Pants.* I wasn't going to let him take this away from me.

"We leave in thirty minutes," he said.

I jumped out of bed and ran to the bathroom to get ready. A second later, I ran back out to him still standing in front of the closet and pressed a quick kiss to his lips to show my appreciation. He was *my* Mr. Grumpy Pants, and his soft interior would do anything to make me happy.

I did a goofy dance, waving my arms in the air, unable to control my excitement. That broke his tough façade, and he gave me the sweetest smile in return. I quickly ran back into the bathroom to hurry before I ran out of time.

Chapter XXIV

Shyam

"How many of those are you going to eat?" I asked.

"They're so good. I need to try all the flavors!" Amelia was inhaling her third *kulfi*, a denser version of ice cream on a stick, flavored with spices or fruit. She seemed to like the mango-flavored one the most, judging from how fervently she licked the cream. My dick noticed and wished it were that *kulfi* in her mouth. "Do you want some?" she asked between licks.

I smirked in response. *Yeah, but not the ice cream.*

She swatted my arm as if reading my thoughts. In a low voice, she said, "Not everything is sexual."

"With me, it is," I said, sneaking a not-so-subtle glance at the cleavage peeking out from under the neckline of her dress.

To spite me, she rearranged the deep-green shawl around her shoulders to cover my prime view. She grinned with satisfaction that she had successfully taken away something that brought me such pleasure.

We continued walking down the outdoor market in downtown Amritsar. We stood out against the sea of people—Amelia with her beautiful red hair and Western features flanked by four of my most intimidating bodyguards. If she noticed that people were staring at us, she didn't let on. She was enraptured by the sights and sounds around her. She was a vision in her flowy yellow dress, embroidered with brightly colored flowers. She insisted on wearing the shawl around her shoulders to blend in with the local women.

A vendor stopped us to show us his display of bracelets in his stall. These shop owners were ruthless with their sales tactics. They aggressively hailed pedestrians, trying to make the most money they could on their goods. I would benefit from hiring a few of them to work for me, with how skilled they were.

I kept walking along, accustomed to ignoring their sales pitches, but soon turned to my side and saw that my partner was missing. She had taken the vendor's bait and was perusing his selection of bangles.

"Shyam, these are so beautiful!" she said, holding up sets of glittering bracelets in either hand. "My mother would love these."

"We'll take six sets of different colors," I said to the vendor in Hindi, handing him a bundle of *rupees*. I wasn't in the mood to haggle with him.

He nodded happily and set about to wrapping and bagging them for us.

"Not those," I said, pointing to the green set that he was about to wrap. Instead, I took them and slipped the set onto her slender forearm. I kissed her wrist before releasing her hand.

"Thank you." She grinned from ear to ear. Her smile lit my heart up like the sun lighting up the world. I would do anything to see it on her face.

I pressed a kiss to her forehead. She lifted her wrist in the air and shook the bangles in elation before walking to another stall.

"Is she your wife, sir?" the vendor asked me as he handed the bag over.

The guy really had no boundaries. "No," I said curtly.

He continued, "If I may offer advice, don't let her go."

I stared at him, unsure of what to say in response.

"The way you look at her, sir. And the way she looks at you. Not many people find that in life."

I nodded at him and said, "Thank you," before turning away.

I had no intention of ever letting her go. But was I ready for marriage? I wasn't against marriage. In fact, I respected its institution. My parents had a great marriage when they were alive. But I had seen what my job could do to the person I loved when my mother was killed, and my father was left alone and heartbroken. I never wanted to bring a woman into this life, destining her to meet the same fate.

I watched her a couple of booths down with two of the guards standing by her. One of the guards seemed to be translating a conversation between her and the vendor. *Another kulfi vendor.* I laughed to myself, finding her obsession adorable. The vendor was all smiles as he offered her a pistachio-flavored ice cream.

Her sweet, carefree attitude was contagious. My house was happier with her in it. My life felt full. Could I really live without her? She was tough. She had proven that when she was kidnapped. Maybe she'd be okay by my side in this life? Certainly, my last name would offer her protection, yet it could also mean her death if someone were pissed enough at me.

Visions of her wearing my wedding ring and round with my child made my heart falter. I could protect her with a fleet of armed men when we went back to New York, but would that be enough? I had so many questions and not enough answers. In fact, I didn't know anything for certain except that I loved her more than anything in this world. I felt so in love yet so frustrated at the same time. I didn't do well when things were out of my control.

She broke my train of thought when she found me with her eyes from in front of the *kulfi* stall. Her eyes twinkled from afar as she smiled and waved her ice cream in the air to show me that she had scored another. I had better get back to her before she made some other men around her horny with the way she was going at her treat. And judging from how she stuffed it between her lips, pistachio was her new favorite.

We walked a little farther, passing by a man seated on the ground playing the *pungi,* a long flute with a large round sphere in the center of it. Amelia stopped to watch the show. The man sat in front of a straw basket with a lid covering it. The loud shrill of his instrument drew a crowd. He removed the lid and the head of cobra rose quickly to peer at its surroundings. Amelia gasped and moved slightly behind me, her head peeking out slightly to continue watching from safety.

The snake charmer continued playing his song, swaying his instrument in front of the reptile. Its hood fully expanded in attack-mode. It stood erect, sizing up its opponent, calculating when to strike. The entire crowd was silent, watching and waiting for the animal to make its first move. The charmer played on, oblivious to the threat before him. The snake began to sway along, matching the movements of the charmer. The man had not only the animal in a trance but the swarm of people standing around him, too.

Suddenly, he stopped playing, removing the music that lightened the spirit of the beast. The snake stopped moving and seemed to remember his need to kill. However, before the cobra could act, the man placed the lid of the basket over the top of the snake's head, gently guiding him back into his basket. The crowd clapped and offered money into a basket next to the man.

Amelia glanced at me, still awestruck at what she had just witnessed.

"Imagine what would have happened if this was a mongoose-snake fight," I said.

She smirked. "The mongoose always wins."

She'd proven that. "Yes, she does."

Chapter XXV

Amelia

I sat in the courtyard enjoying the early morning sunshine on a patch of grass with a book I had found in the library. *Rikki-Tikki-Tavi* by Rudyard Kipling. It was about a mongoose taken in as a pet by a British family living in India, and the mongoose protected them from cobras.

The sun seemed to be getting hotter earlier every day, so I was only able to get out shortly after breakfast to enjoy the fresh air. My skin was naturally sensitive to sun, burning easily anytime I was out for too long, so I was always sure to be armed with lots of sunscreen and a hat.

I wasn't alone this morning. A couple of women from the kitchen staff sat on a blanket a bit away from me busy preparing food while chatting in Hindi. The kitchen staff consisted of both older and younger women who prepared all our meals. This morning, the younger women were present, which was also probably why there was more talking than working going on.

I abandoned my book and walked over to them. One of the ladies looked up at me, startled that I was hovering over them. "Hi, there. Mind if I help you?" I asked.

The ladies looked at each other. "Miss, I don't think that would be appropriate," she answered looking anxious, as if she were about to get in trouble for talking to me.

I didn't understand the reason for formalities, but I knew that there was some sort of line that house staff weren't supposed to cross in this culture. However, I was screwing their boss, so I would make sure no one would get in trouble.

I sat down on the blanket. They had dishes of various grains and lentils in the middle. They continued with their work in silence. I watched their nimble fingers weed through the contents of the dishes, picking out pebbles, husks, and anything else that was inedible. I grabbed one of the large dishes and followed suit. Quiet gasps came from them as I copied them and plucked out impurities.

I ignored their surprise and worked through my dish of rice. "I've never done this before," I admitted.

"Let me know if I'm doing this properly."

The older of the girls, the one closest to me, reluctantly passed me a small dish to deposit my pebbles. "Thanks," I said gratefully. She was beautiful, with dark, shiny hair and smooth skin. She wore minimal makeup and had a small, jeweled stud on the side of her nose. I noticed that most of the women here had their noses pierced.

The amount of food before me was unbelievable. "Will all of this be prepared for tonight's dinner?" I asked incredulously.

The older woman, who was about my age, answered, "No, we prepare all of this in advance so it's ready when we need it for cooking."

The younger girl, no more than sixteen years old, added, "Although, at the rate Master Jai has been having guests over, we'll burn through this supply in a week." The older one gasped in shock at her boldness. The girl seemed embarrassed of her own honesty and diverted her gaze to the dish of yellow lentils in front of her.

I ignored their reactions and continued cleaning out my dish of rice. "I believe it! Jai is a party animal. The other night, we had a dinner party, and he had an afterparty at his place with lord knows who else."

They both giggled. "I'm Nadia, by the way," said the outspoken girl.

"Nice to meet you. I'm Amelia." I was sure they knew all about me since I was familiar with the staff's affinity for gossip. I couldn't understand most of what they said since they mostly spoke in another language, but I could make out a few random words Shyam had uttered before and my name.

She nodded and smiled. "This is my sister Nalini." She motioned to the woman next to her. "She is madly in love with Master Jai."

Nalini dropped her mouth open and smacked her sister on the arm for telling her secrets. "*Chup!*" *Shut up!* Nalini's cheeks were bright red from the shame of being outed.

I laughed. "It's okay. I understand. He's got a charm about him."

Nadia ducked her head shyly. She looked on either side of her to make sure no one else was around and leaned in toward me. "I see lots of women in his apartment really late at night," she whispered.

"Nadia, be quiet!" Nalini admonished her sister. She seemed panicked that I would get upset. "I'm so sorry about my sister. She talks too much."

"I won't say anything. I promise."

One of the elder women from the kitchen shouted for Nalini to come back to the house to help with something. She must have not seen me helping them because she didn't scold Nalini.

Nalini stood up, towering over her sister. "You be good. And don't run your mouth while I'm gone."

Nadia exhaled a sigh of relief as her sister walked off. She rolled her eyes. "Big sisters."

I smiled.

"Is it true?" she asked.

"Is what true?"

"That in America, Master Jai has a houseful of women that he keeps on hand for his…needs?"

I bit back my smile. I hadn't been over to Jai's house in New York, so I didn't know for sure if it were true, but the idea of Jai having an in-house harem made me want to laugh. "I don't think he keeps a staff of women ready and waiting for him."

"I told Nalini that if she's not careful, she could turn into one of those girls," she whispered.

I loved Jai, but he went through women like they were disposable, and I wouldn't advise any self-respecting woman to be involved with his wild parties. "I think Nalini is smarter than to get mixed up in something like that."

She continued picking at her bowl of lentils. "My sister is pretty smart, but she's obsessed with him. She won't stop pining over him."

"Well, maybe she should just say 'hello' and become friends with Jai first," I said, even though I knew Jai wasn't really a relationship kind of a guy.

"Master Jai is not the type of man that women are *friends* with. He uses them." Nadia had seen through my lie. Her perception was on point.

"I don't think he's that bad." At least, I hoped he would settle down one day.

"I see the women who stay in his apartment overnight," she said, her eyes widening because she was excited to share some gossip.

I laughed. I liked this girl. She was brutally honest. "You spy on him?"

"Um—not spy. No. Just *observe.*" She leaned in closer to me to whisper in my ear, "They barely wear clothes."

Oh lord. I didn't want to hear this. It was like hearing about your brother with strippers.

"They wear sexy *sarees* showing their cleavage and bellies. And it drives all the men crazy. Sometimes Master Jai has no clothes on and has *two* girls on his lap at the same time." She seemed so proud of herself for knowing all of this.

Gross! I needed to gouge my eyes out from the visual. I couldn't hide the look of appall on my face.

"No, don't worry, Mistress Amelia. Master Shyam is never there anymore. The other maids say he used to be before he met you, but never since you came along. He's a good person. Very respectful from what I've seen."

I knew she was telling the truth because he was with me whenever he wasn't working. I knew he had a past and had probably participated in some of the extracurricular activities that his bachelor brother partook in. However, I was secure enough to know that he didn't miss them. Not from how he handled me in bed.

I had an idea on how to treat my man to a little experience from his old life.

"Hey, Nadia. I wonder if you could help me with something—for Master Shyam?"

"For you? Anything!" she exclaimed.

Poor girl didn't know what she was getting herself into.

Chapter XXVI

Shyam

I checked the clock on my laptop. Eleven o'clock. I had spent longer than I intended finishing up some accounts that I had started earlier in the day. I felt guilty for rushing through dinner with Amelia to get back to my office to work. She hadn't seemed offended by it and said she wanted to finish reading her book. *Rikki-Tikki-Tavi.* Lord knows why, of all the works of literature in the library, she had chosen a children's book to read.

I turned the lights out in my office and closed the door on my way out. She was probably waiting for me in bed since it was late. Just knowing that she was lying in bed in her panties and one of my t-shirts, ready for me to slide inside of her, made my dick twitch. I took the stairs up to my room, two at a time, in a hurry to get to her.

The top buttons of my shirt felt constricting as my blood ran hot with arousal. I unbuttoned them as I pushed my bedroom door in, excitement coursing through my veins.

I was surprised when I found our bed still made and Amelia not in it. I checked the bathroom and then the closet to see if maybe she was changing her clothes in there. *Nothing.*

I wondered if maybe she had gone for a late-night snack and I had missed her in the kitchen when I came upstairs. I went back down to the first floor and turned on the kitchen light. The kitchen was spotless and packed up for the night. *"Jaan?"* No answer.

It was odd that she'd be wandering the house this late.

I heard a soft rustling noise down the hall. I followed it to the music room. It was one of the rooms my mother had loved the most in this house. She had been an avid musician and played all different types of instruments, from the piano to the sitar. She had collected many one-of-a-kind instruments and set up the room to be her own personal music studio to experiment with sounds and teach Jai and me to play various instruments.

The door was ajar, which was alarming since no one used this room anymore. I played piano but rarely ever found time to practice these days. The maids were the only ones who went in there to dust.

My pulse quickened on alert. I knew something was off. I didn't have my gun on me, and I was cursing myself for it.

There was a panic button in the room, so I could always press that if needed and the guards would be there in seconds.

I pushed the door open slowly. White candles of varying sizes illuminated the room. The moonlight from the large window in the far end of the room also provided soft lighting. I looked around, and that's when I saw her, looking like a goddess—my *jaan*. All the air left my lungs when I saw her.

Glittering jewels adorned her ears and the middle part of her hair. Gold bangles decorated her wrists. Her sea of red hair flowed in soft waves around her shoulders. She wore the fabric that draped over her body with the air of a queen. *My queen.*

The silk blouse clung to curves of her chest, only stopping right under her breasts. Sheer material, like fine-knit lace, fell across her abdomen in a thin strip in a way I had only seen in erotic paintings. The skin on her belly was exposed and begging for my caress. The bottom part of her *saree* was wrapped into loose harem-style pants that hung low on her hips. Any lower and I would see the faint proof auburn path of hair that would lead me to heaven. Her feet were bare, with shiny anklets hugging her ankles. *Holy fuck.* I could cum right now just looking at her.

Heavily lined green eyes stared back at me with desire that burned my blood. She must have noticed my jaw on the floor because her full lips were pressed into the most seductive smirk. I was hers and she knew it.

215

She stepped closer to me, her hips swaying from side to side, her movements accentuated by the flow of fabric. I was frozen to my spot, unable to move or even speak, as she took the lead.

Her hands ran down the front of my shirt, feeling my chest through the crisp cotton. Scents of jasmine and vanilla enveloped me as she moved in closer.

I swallowed the lump in my throat before speaking. "You look so goddamn beautiful." *That was an understatement.* I wasn't a man of many words, but I truly couldn't find the right words in this moment.

She smiled slyly as she undid the rest of my shirt buttons, painfully slow. "I can't take all the credit. I had help from your kitchen maid, Nadia," she said, focusing intently on each button as she disarmed it.

"Remind me to give Nadia a raise later," I whispered.

I pulled her chin up with my finger until her gaze met my eyes. Beyond the lust and the passion, I could see the woman that I was meant to spend the rest of my life with.

"Stay with me forever, *jaan.*"

Her breath caught as she absorbed my request. A nod was the only sign of her promise.

"I want to spend the rest of my life with you." I wanted her by my side, raising a family together.

Like her jewels, her eyes glittered as tears formed in them from such hope and adoration.

I held her face in my hands. "This isn't a proposal. I will do this properly, but do know that I want it."

She couldn't hold back the tears leaking from the corners of her eyes. "That's all I ever needed. Just to know."

I couldn't wait to feel her lips anymore. Our mouths moved together—carefully coordinated movements connecting our souls. Her tongue danced with mine, following my lead. The fire we created consumed us, making us need for more. Our breaths grew ragged as desperation took hold.

I pulled my shirt off and threw it aside as she worked the fly of my pants. As much as I wanted to continue to feast on the sight of her in a *saree*, I needed to feel her naked against me. I tugged on the bunch of lace across her belly, causing it to fall loose from her shoulders. Usually, women pinned the shit out of these outfits to keep them in place, but she had known I'd be ripping it off and had forgone the task. Yards of white unraveled around her body and fell into a puddle on the floor.

Panties, like the pins, had also been left out, too. *Fuck, she knows me well.* She stood only in her blouse and the jewels that adorned her body. My eyes roamed down to the flesh between her legs that I was so desperate to feel but caught something in their view on the way. A glimmer of light on her belly button. I leaned in closer for a better look.

"Do you like it?" she asked nervously.

"Is it real?" I asked as I massaged the stone with my fingertip.

217

She chuckled. "No. It's a clip-on. Nadia said it 'drives the men wild.'"

I growled in approval. "Remind me to buy Nadia a fucking car when we're done." I quickly stood up and lifted her with me. She squealed, wrapping her legs around my waist. I grabbed her lips between mine and continued my assault on her mouth. Her arms wrapped around my neck and her hands clutched my hair as I carried her across the room. I sat her on a massive drum by the window. The moonlight irradiated her bright eyes in the dark room. She was the only light I needed to see clearly.

I kicked off my shoes and removed my socks with my eyes glued to hers. My pants and boxers came off next, allowing my cock to rise freely to offer its prayer to the goddess before it.

She undid the clasps on the front of her blouse, freeing the round globes that my mouth watered for. I had thought lingerie was the sexiest clothing on a woman before now. I made a mental note to buy her more *sarees*.

I grabbed a nipple between my teeth and pulled on it, causing her to yelp in surprise. I sucked on the little point to ease the harshness of my rough treatment.

Her legs hooked around my ass, pulling me closer to her. She licked a trail on my chest between my nipples. I pushed her back to lay flat on the drum and knelt before her pussy. It glistened with arousal in the moonlight. I stroked my tongue from her asshole up to her slit. Her hips bucked in the air and slammed back down onto the surface of the drum, causing a deep *thump* to reverberate. I pushed harder on her sternum to keep her from moving. My tongue worked circles on her clitoris, eliciting loud moans from her throat. Her legs wrapped around my head, locking me in front of her wet folds. With each swipe of my tongue, I moved lower, tasting her essence. *Silky honey.* A man could get drunk off her sweetness.

More liquid spilled from her depths. Her hips circled in time with my tongue, pushing into my face more with each rotation. I removed my hand from her chest, allowing her back to arch of its own free will. My fingers pulled her lips apart to allow my tongue to sink in to drink from her fountain. My fingers gave her the friction she loved so much on her clit, drawing out tight circles. Her hips bucked in response and her fingers found my hair, holding on tight. Beautiful screams filled my ears as she found her release, spilling her nectar into my mouth.

When her body came down from her high and settled, I continued to lap at her folds, making her squirm from sensitivity.

My dick required attention immediately. The pain was blinding. "Roll onto your side," I commanded.

She listened and rolled into a ball on her side. Her bottom arm was extended flat on the surface of the drum supporting the side of her head and her the palm of her other hand gently rested flat to provide her extra support. I lifted her upper thigh slightly to separate her lower lips to make room for me. My cock did all the thinking on his own, lining himself up with her entrance. My hips drove forward, sliding my length into its safe space. I groaned as she squeezed around me. She felt so tight in this position, liken it was the first time her pussy had ever been fucked. I moved unapologetically, not even stopping to acclimate her to my size. With each plunge, my balls slapped against the piece of flesh where the bottom of her ass cheek met the top of her thigh.

Her hip beat against the drum as she took each pump. Rhythmic *thumps* created a song that filled the room. The tinkling of her anklets added to the melody. Our moans mixed with panting breaths provided the chorus. My pace quickened as I felt my cock go rigid. I drove us home, our cries of ecstasy finishing off our symphony of pleasure. My seed spilled into her warmth, continuing long after we found our edge.

We stayed connected like that for a while, never wanting these feelings to end. I leaned over her body and found her lips with mine.

We had said "I love you" so many times since she returned to me, but right now, our eyes spoke for us. No words were good enough to express how we truly felt. We didn't need them. For the first time in my life, I was with someone who knew exactly how I felt, and felt the same way about me, too.

CHAPTER XXVII

SHYAM

"What was so important that you had to drag me out of bed this early in the morning?" I was pissed hearing my phone go off after a glorious night of mind-blowing fucking all over my house. Amelia was a fucking wet dream come to life and I kept blowing my load like a teenage boy first discovering how to jack off. I should have been back in bed with her, pounding into her until cum dripped out of her cunt. Instead, I was here with my stupid-ass brother in the office.

"We have a problem," he replied, opening his laptop on my desk.

"You bet your fucking ass, we do. I'm going to shove my shoe up your asshole for disturbing me." I hadn't even had my morning coffee yet.

"Russians," he said.

"What?" He really was asking for an ass-kicking if he was going to speak in one-word riddles.

He continued, "Tarun was heavily involved with the Russian mafia."

We knew this. Russia had always been Tarun's territory, and now that he was out of the picture, we controlled it. "This isn't news."

"They're involved in human trafficking." His face was fixed into a pained expression as if it should have upset me.

Again, we knew this. Jai and I only dealt with drugs, but our various clients dabbled in all sorts of criminal departments like weapon sales or even human trafficking. However, that didn't mean we were touching any of those extracurriculars. "You dragged me out of bed to tell me this? I really am going to beat the shit out of you."

"Shut up and listen. They were going to take Amelia." He pointed to his computer.

My blood ran cold. I stared at his computer screen in disbelief. The electronic file with all the information needed by the Russians to secure her was right in front of me. I was going to be sick.

"Tarun struck a deal with them to sell her for top dollar after he succeeded in taking over our business. When he didn't need her anymore, he was going to trade her for the money."

I was barely able to speak because I was in shock. "How did you find this out?" I managed to whisper.

"I have an informant on the inside of Russian operations," he said.

The same rage I had felt when I knew Tarun took her spread through my body. My knuckles went white from how hard I clenched my fists in my lap.

"Tarun is dead and we're in charge of their supply now. So, this isn't a problem anymore." I knew I was speaking a lie as soon as I said it; otherwise, Jai wouldn't have called for an urgent meeting.

Judging from the grim look on Jai's face, I was right. His shoulders sulked with pity before he answered. "They still want payment. It's her or money."

There was no question about what the choice would be. I would pay any amount of money to keep her safe. "How much do they want?"

Jai swallowed the lump in his throat. His Adam's apple bobbed with how nervous he was. "One hundred and fifty million dollars."

I nearly fell out of my chair. "What the fuck?! They were going to pay that much for her?" I choked out.

"No, of course not. They said that they still wanted her or to be 'reasonably compensated for their inconvenience.'"

Of course, they did. *Greedy bastards.*

I didn't like being taken advantage of, especially by thirsty assholes like the Russians, but the decision was clear for me. "Then give them the money."

Jai looked at me seriously. "Shyam, that's a lot of money."

I launched myself at him, grabbing him by his collar. "Are you fucking serious? Are you really going to have me consider giving her up instead of the money?"

"No, man!" he blurted out quickly. "I love that girl! She's my fucking sister! I'm just saying that it's a lot of money and we just recovered the business, so things are tight right now."

I let go of his shirt to consider what he'd said. It was true. We had the money saved up, but income from the business wasn't flowing fast enough to make up for that kind of loss.

"We're giving them the money," I said with finality.

"What if we worked out a deal with them?" Jai asked, rubbing his neck where his shirt had cut into his skin when I yanked him.

"With the Brotherhood?" They were not known for their ability to compromise.

"Yeah, maybe we could offer them a price cut on all product we provide to them?"

I considered it for a moment. "That could work. Do you think they'd go for it?"

"I don't know," Jai said. "They're unpredictable. I could ask my informant to feel it out for us."

"Contact him now," I demanded. I needed this to be cleared up immediately so Amelia would be safe as soon as possible.

He shook his head. "It doesn't work that fast. I'd need to explain our proposal to my inside guy, and he would need time to test out their response."

"How much time?" We didn't have time to sit on this. I needed a solution now.

"Days or even weeks," he answered apologetically.

That was too long when it came to ensuring her safety. "What happens to her in the meantime?"

His expression turned regretful. "She can't stay with us. She's not safe until we finalize a deal. At this point, we're not even sure they'll accept what we offer them."

"That's stupid," I argued. "She's safest with me," I shouted pointing to my chest.

"No. She's only worth something to them if she's worth something to you."

"Are you asking me to send her away?" I couldn't believe he was expecting me to send away the only woman I had ever genuinely loved. It took me so long to admit my true feelings for her, and now I had to let her go?

He moved around the desk and took a seat facing me. "I know it's not an easy decision to make, but it's for her own protection."

"No. I will not do it." I had just promised her the world last night. I had promised to make her my wife and grow old with her, and now Jai was expecting me to rescind my commitment to her?

"You have to do this. She's not safe if she's associated with you. Look at how her ties to us got her to India in the first place."

I pressed my fingers to the bridge of my nose to steady the migraine that was spreading over my head. Or maybe it was to hold back the tears of frustration that I wanted to shed.

Jai pressed his fingertips together, resting them under his chin. "Show them that she's meaningless to you and we can work on cutting their fees for extra security."

"But won't they suspect that she still means something to me if we cut their fees?"

He shrugged. "Maybe, but we can also give them exclusive rights to conduct their business in the North. They're constantly fighting between borders for control of the area. We can give them what they want by charging neighboring countries more to sweeten the pot."

I frowned. "That will piss off the Serbs and Ukrainians." I would bend over backwards to protect Amelia but starting a Slavic war didn't sound like a good move either.

"Their sales are much lower than the Russians. And we don't have a choice. We need to play nice The Brotherhood right now," he said.

He was right. They were smart as fuck and they'd take a deal like this if it gave them more power over their neighbors and cheaper costs for our goods so they could jack up the price and overtake territory previously owned by other countries. It was a dangerous game but anything involving the Russians was dangerous.

I shut my eyes tightly, exhausted from the wave of emotions I felt and the decision I had to make. "I guess that's it, then? I have to send her away," I said quietly. My heart had been ripped out and there was no light when I thought of a life without her.

Jai looked at me, unable to hide his pity. "It's for the best. You're keeping her safe. Remember how you felt when Tarun took her? This time, you get to save her before she's in danger again. You can prevent it."

I pressed my hand to the center of my chest trying to ease the pain inside. "If that's supposed to bring me relief, then why does it feel like I can't breathe?"

He got up from his chair and walked over to me. He put a hand on my slumped shoulders. "Because—you're in *love*."

Chapter XXVIII

Amelia

I woke up to a deliciously sore feeling from the night I'd had. I smiled, remembering it all. His touch. His words. His promise. *"This isn't a proposal. I will do this properly, but do know that I want it."*

He wanted to marry me. We hadn't discussed the details, but he did want a future with me. I couldn't imagine myself with anyone else for the rest of my life. My heart swelled every time I pictured us married in a house together, with lots of children and maybe a puppy or two.

Our relationship wasn't the only thing that had changed; he had changed too. He was no longer afraid of commitment and had let down his guard, trusting me with his emotions.

I reached over to feel for the man who had made love to me until I was too tired to take anymore. His part of the bed was cold, like he had been gone for a while. After the night, and part of the early morning, that we'd had, I would have expected him to be as exhausted as I was and sleep in.

I needed a strong cup of coffee. My stomach grumbled as I stood up and stretched. I needed food too. Lots of food. I usually ate a light breakfast, if even at all, but today I was in the mood for something warm and fried that Raj tried to push on me every morning. I decided I should freshen up first before heading down so I didn't wreak of sex while talking to the kitchen staff.

My reflection in the bathroom mirror was comical. Hair every which way. Black eye makeup smeared around my face. Stupidly happy grin.

Shyam wasn't the only one who had changed in this relationship. I had changed too. I was no longer the quiet pushover that he first met. I felt confident in my own skin and assertive enough to hold my own against this strong and powerful man. Before, I would have been mortified if a man ever saw me like this, but now, I didn't care. It was probably cliché but being in love felt so freeing.

I opted for a quick shower and changed into a flowy pink maxi dress before setting out to search for food.

After freshening up, I entered the bustling kitchen. "Good morning, Raj."

He was a large man with a warm smile. "Good morning, ma'am. May I get you your usual coffee this morning?"

"Yes, please. Also, I was wondering if you had anything for breakfast?"

"Of course. What would you like?" He clasped his hands in front of his waist, expecting to hear my order of something light like toast or cereal.

"What was that thing you offered me yesterday?" I looked up to the ceiling trying to think of what it was called. "Bread stuffed with potatoes?"

Raj hesitated, as if he had heard incorrectly. "*Aloo puri*?"

I snapped my fingers with excitement. "Yes, that's it!"

His face beamed at my request. The man lived to serve, and I could tell I had just made his day. "Of course, ma'am." He bowed to me. "Right away. Have a seat and I'll bring it for you."

I took a seat at the table. Raj quickly set a coffee cup down in front of me.

"Thank you so much," I said.

"You're welcome, ma'am. I'll be right back with your breakfast," he said, turning away quickly to retrieve the food.

I stopped him before he could leave. "By the way, have you seen Shyam this morning?"

231

"I believe he is in an important meeting with Master Jai, ma'am."

Hmmm. I hope nothing is wrong. He was still busy with organizing the business, but he had never let me know that anything was wrong. Maybe it was just another mini fire that needed his attention. Nothing that he and Jai couldn't handle, I hoped.

"Oh, okay. Thank you." He hurried back to the kitchen in excitement to prepare my meal.

After a long and very filling breakfast, I wandered into the library to find another book. I had finished my book about the mongoose. It was entertaining for a children's book, but now I was in the mood for something more risqué after the night I'd had. Unfortunately, there were no sexy novels on the any of the shelves. I settled on *Jane Eyre*, a classic. I knew it by heart, but never tired of re-reading it.

Book in hand, I wandered down the hall to make my way to the courtyard for some fresh air. I passed by Shyam's office on the way. I missed my man, but I respected that he was busy working. I could probably pop in for a quick kiss and be on my way. I was sure he wouldn't mind.

I knocked on the door. I heard voices from inside and then some shuffling of shoes. A moment later, the door opened. Jai poked his head out. Judging from his expression, he was less than excited to see me. He looked back into the office before stepping completely into the hallway, closing the door behind him.

"Hey, doll. What's up?" he asked, avoiding eye contact.

"You're up early," I teased.

"You know—early bird gets—ummm—some shit or another." Something was off. He wasn't his usual vibrant self. He seemed ready to run away just to avoid me.

I raised my eyebrow at him. "Is everything okay?"

"Yeah, why wouldn't it be?" he answered hastily.

"Is Shyam in there?" I motioned to the door he guarded.

"Shyam?" he asked vacantly, as if he had no recollection of who I was referring to.

"Yeah, you know. Your brother?" What the hell was going on?

He chuckled nervously. "Oh, yeah. He's on a phone call."

"Oh." I knew he was lying. I didn't hear Shyam's deep voice behind the door, so there was no way he was on the phone. "I just wanted to say hi."

"I'll relay the message." He fixed his mouth into a forced smile.

"Are you sure everything's okay?"

"Yeah, he's just busy. Got plans for the day?" He was trying to distract me.

"Not really. I was just going to head outside and read a book." I waved my book in the air.

"Oh. Wonderful. Well, don't let me keep you." He pressed his hand on my upper back and gently guided me in the direction of the courtyard doors. Why was he trying to get rid of me?

"Um—okay. See ya." I walked away slowly. That was the most awkward interaction I had ever had with Jai.

***

I spent the entire day alone. It was nearly five o'clock in the evening and I hadn't seen Shyam yet. Dinner would be in a few hours and I wasn't sure if he'd surface by then. Sitting in a leather armchair in the library, I continued thumbing through the pages of my book, not really reading any of the words that usually offered me comfort with their familiarity. Everything seemed foreign to me, even this book.

I kept replaying the events of last night, and I couldn't think of anything that would have upset him. Had I said something in my sleep that set him off? I was grasping at straws to find a reason why he was ignoring me.

Maybe I was just being silly. Most often, the simplest answer was the right one. It had to be something with work. He was probably was just busy with work.

Raj's voice interrupted my thoughts. "Ma'am, Master Shyam would like to see you in the office."

234

This felt too formal to me. Why couldn't he just come get me himself? However, I was too anxious to see him to spend another moment fussing over this small of a detail.

I sprang to my feet and walked hurriedly down to his office. My heart was racing, and my hand shook as I knocked on the door.

Something was wrong; I just knew it before he even answered. "Come in."

I entered, scared of what I would find inside.

The office was dimly lit. Shyam was behind his desk, his eyes trained on the papers on his desk.

I closed the door behind me. The room was silent except for the sound of my sandals on the hard marble as I cautiously approached the front of the desk.

He didn't speak or even look up at me.

"Hey," I tried to break the tension, my voice heavy with concern.

"Have a seat," he replied bluntly. No emotion—just to the point.

His demeanor was troubling. This wasn't like the man I had known just twenty-four hours ago. That man was warm and loving. No. This was the man I had met in New York—cold and clinical. This was the man who took over my old company and refused to commit to me.

I didn't listen to his order because I was too nervous to sit down. "What's wrong?"

He finally looked up from his desk, his eyes holding mine. They were bloodshot and dark circles framed them, showing signs of stress and worry.

I walked quickly around the desk to his chair. "Babe. What happened?"

He stopped me before I could reach out and touch his face. He held out a sheet of paper in front of me, keeping me from getting closer to him.

"What's this?" I asked, taking the paper from him.

He didn't answer.

I read it, trying hard to get my eyes to focus on the words instead of listening to the storm of thoughts in my head. I only made it as far as the heading before I spoke. "A letter of recommendation?"

He nodded.

I didn't understand. All these dramatics just for the letter of recommendation that I had asked for when I first agreed to help him track down Tarun?

"Um—thanks. Are you upset with me because I plan to use this to leave Sethi Tech?" If he wanted me to stay, he just had to tell me.

"No. I want you to leave."

It had always been my plan to find an even better job one day, at another tech company, using this letter to help me. He knew this too, but hearing him say that he wanted me to leave crushed something inside of me. It was the way he said it—so detached, like he wanted me to leave forever.

"I'm not in a hurry to find a new job," I said. "Maybe when we go back to New York, I'll start looking for—"

He cut me off before I could finish, his tone final. "You're not going back to New York."

I frowned. "What do you mean?"

He handed me another document. A flight itinerary. I stared at the three capital letters of the destination airport in shock. The combination of sharp black ink and the emotionless font of the letters on the white bill mocked me.

The words came out as a whisper, hoping that it wasn't true and that I was seeing things. "This says I'm going to Seattle—tomorrow?"

"I've notified my on-call flight crew and they will take you home tomorrow afternoon," he said, dry like the words on the paper.

"Are you coming with me?" I asked hopefully. None of this made sense.

He hesitated before answering. "No. I'm going back to New York—without you."

237

Realization dawned on me, knocking the air out of my lungs. "Are you breaking up with me?"

He diverted his eyes from mine, confirming my question.

My knees were ready to give out under me. I placed a hand on his desk to support myself. "I don't understand," I whispered. "Everything was fine yesterday and last night was amazing. Did I do something wrong?"

He exhaled a deep breath before meeting my eyes again. Regret washed over his face. "No, *jaan*. You didn't do anything wrong."

"Then why are you pushing me away like a coward?" My voice grew loud with frustration. "Was everything you promised me last night just pillow talk?"

"God, no. I meant those things." He stared at me dead in my eyes to prove to me that his words were true.

"Then what is it?" I shouted. "Because I'm not getting it."

He clenched his eyes tightly before answering. "You're not safe with me."

Of course, I was. We were safest together. "Why not?"

He shook his head. "I can't say. You just need to go."

I was infuriated. Rage took over my tongue. "After all I've been through for you and your business, and you can't give me an explanation as to why I need to leave? This is bullshit!" I threw my hands in the air, because I was fucking fed up with this merry-go-round of a conversation.

He stood up and moved to put his hand on my arm to comfort me. I pulled away in disgust. "Don't fucking touch me."

"Please, *jaan*," he begged. "This is for your own good."

"Stop making decisions for me. I thought we had moved on from you bossing me around and deciding my future. I can make my own decisions. In case you didn't realize it, I'm a big girl who killed *your* fucking enemy." I was screaming so loud that my throat hurt, but I didn't care about the pain.

"This isn't the same thing, I—"

I interrupted him, "Then explain it to me. Oh wait—*you can't,*" I shouted, mocking his voice.

"My hands are tied." His voice was quiet. Too quiet. I wanted him to yell or cry or curse at me just to know that he was feeling just as frustrated as me.

"You're a pussy. I fucking hate you." My hands started flailing, hitting his chest relentlessly. He grabbed my hands to stop me, and I couldn't hold back the tears any longer. They came pouring out as I sobbed.

He held me as I mourned the loss of him. I felt like I was at his funeral even though I was still wrapped in his arms. "Why won't you trust me?" I whispered through my tears.

His chin rested on the top of my head. "I do trust you. I just don't trust anyone else when it comes to you."

***

I didn't remember how I had gotten here, but I was curled up in the fetal position in bed—his bed. I felt like crying some more, but the tears wouldn't come. I was numb. It felt like when he first told me he didn't believe in settling down but so much worse. This time, I felt like I had been stabbed in the gut and left to bleed out.

I didn't even know what time it was. I could have been lying here for minutes or even hours for all I knew. My flight was in the afternoon, but I didn't care at all about packing. I didn't have anything here anyway. Not anymore.

I felt the bed dip next to me. The body that had once brought me security was no longer enough to warm me. The strong arm that had once grounded me no longer kept my thoughts from spiraling dizzily in my head. The steady breath on the back of my neck that had once soothed me to sleep no longer calmed me. I wanted to get up and run away from all of it, but my body wouldn't move.

His lips pressed to the back of my head. "I'm sorry," he whispered into my hair. My tears fell again on cue and my body shuddered with my sobs.

He rolled me over, so my back was flat on the bed, and he propped his body up on his arm to look down into my eyes. "*Jaan*. I love you." He tried to dry my tears with his fingers, but it was useless because they wouldn't stop streaming down my face.

I was done screaming and yelling to try to reason with him. There was nothing he could say to make this right. If he didn't trust me enough to give me an explanation, then I had to leave. But it didn't make it any easier to say goodbye.

His lips met mine and I could finally exhale fully. My brain told me to resist, but my heart wouldn't listen. My lips parted, giving him permission to take more of my soul than I should logically give. Maybe it was because I wanted a bit more of his in return, to keep with me when I left.

Our kisses were numbered, and we treated this one like it was our last, pouring everything we had left to give into our lips. Our tongues explored each other's mouths for the last time, bidding each other farewell through their embrace.

He moved down to my neck, tasting my fallen tears on the way. Each press of his lips against my skin held contact longer than the last, as if he were memorizing the feel of my skin beneath him. Breathy moans escaped my mouth as he moved lower, between my breasts. His once steady fingers were now shaky and uncertain when they unbuttoned my sleep shirt. My fingers grasped the sides of his face as he explored the skin he had just revealed with his mouth, begging him to never give up on me. His mouth found my nipple and sucked gently, making my body writhe under his hold. His tongue traveled down the length of my breast to my rib. I couldn't help the moans that left me of their own volition. My head might have hated him, but my body would never stop loving him.

He lifted off me, pulling the hem of his shirt over his head and tossing it aside. My gaze settled on his chest. The chiseled pecs that were hard enough to force the most sinister of enemies to the ground when displaying the true force of his strength. Yet, they weren't strong enough to protect me from whatever evil he feared on my behalf.

Wrapping my arms around his neck, I tugged him closer to me so my lips could lace kisses on his skin. My mouth moved over to his nipple. I bit down hard, causing him to groan from pain. I wanted him to feel agony, just like the agony he was putting me through. I slid lower down to his abs, making a path with my bites, each one harder than the last. He flinched from the pain, but it didn't bring me any satisfaction. Nothing would ease my heavy heart, not even revenge.

He gently pushed me back down, to stop my assault. My hands flew upward, ready to fight him, nails ready to claw at him to make him suffer. With one hand, he grabbed both my wrists and pinned them over my head to the mattress—his grip squeezing so tightly that I'd have bruises to remember him by. Even in our rawest moments, we fought each other for control.

His other hand pushed my panties down. I kicked them off, freeing my legs from restraint. He worked his pants and boxers down enough to free the only part of him that was unapologetic for the pain it would cause me—the only pain that I wanted to experience right now. Without hesitating, he pushed his cock in until my swollen lips slapped against the base, causing us to groan and grunt in unison. All my aching thoughts ceased their torment on my brain. This feeling was the drug I needed to cure my depression.

His hand never left my wrists as he retracted and plunged into me over and over again. My knees fell apart, opening for him even more. I bridged my hips up slightly, forcing him to hit the sweet spot on my front inner wall. His head massaged that special area with each potent stroke. His pants huffed out in desperation as his speed quickened. With each pump into me, his expression mirrored the torture he felt inside. Torture from the need to feel more of me, to make this last. Torture over his decision to push me away.

My hips ground against him, matching his frenetic momentum. My need for release matched my need to draw this out. I never wanted this to be over. In the end, my body betrayed me, just like Shyam had betrayed me, slipping one foot over the edge of the cliff. Gravity took over, yanking me into the abyss. Violent screams left my body as I thrashed against the lightning that ripped inside of me, sending electricity coursing through veins. My body contorted off the mattress as if I had been electrocuted. The tensity of my muscles bearing down on his length sent Shyam thundering into the storm with me.

His body collapsed onto mine as we gasped for air without really finding the cleansing breaths we needed to center us.

When the high wore off, I remembered what had gotten us here. Wordlessly, I rolled over onto my side with my back facing him, curling back into the ball he had found me in. He spooned me from behind until my eyes closed and the room slipped into darkness one final time.

***

"Ma'am, the car is ready for you," Raj said from outside the bedroom door.

"I'll be out soon," I shouted so he wouldn't offer to come inside to help me. I wanted to be alone.

I didn't have any belongings here, except the snake pendant that I wore around my neck. It was pretty much all I had come to India with in the first place. I refused to take any of the clothes that Shyam had given me. I had one small carry-on bag with the bracelets Shyam bought for me at the market, which I was planning on giving to my mom as souvenirs. It would seem strange if I showed up empty handed if I were supposed to be willfully returning from a work trip. I had also tucked the letter of recommendation he had given me into a small pocket at the front of my bag. I hadn't checked my email since I had been here, but I was sure an electronic copy was waiting in my inbox. Shyam had insisted that I take the cellphone he had given me too. I didn't decline since I needed one in case of emergency on my way to Seattle.

I looked around the bedroom one last time. Soon after I left, the maids would clean up and remove any evidence of my time here. The next woman to grace this room would never know that I existed. My stomach churned at the thought of someone else sharing his bed.

To stop this destructive cascade of suspicion, I grabbed my bag and left the room without looking back.

I made way to the bottom of the stairs, where several staff members waited in a line. One of the men took my bag out to the car for me.

Nadia was the first to approach me. Instead of a polite goodbye or handshake, she grabbed me into a tight hug. "Goodbye, Nadia. You take care of yourself," I said as I hugged her back.

"Goodbye, Mistress Amelia," she said with tears in her eyes.

I held her face in my hands and smiled as I looked into her innocent eyes, "Stay out of trouble. No more spying on...*people*." She glanced at Jai from the side and nodded in agreement.

Her sister was more polite and composed, offering me a handshake.

I moved down the line to Raj. He moved to bow to me, but I stopped him before he could. I pulled him into a hug. "Thank you for everything," I whispered, fighting back more tears. Why did I have to be such a damn crier about anything emotional?

He cupped my face in his hand. "You are most welcome, my dear. Please take care of yourself and remember to eat well."

I nodded. "I'll try, but nothing can beat your food."

He smiled in response, letting me go.

Jai was the last in the line. He knew the real reason I was being forced to leave but refused to tell me anything in solidarity with his brother. I was upset with him too, but I couldn't hold it against him. Siblings *should* stick together.

He wrapped me up in a tight hug and kissed the side of my head. "You take care of yourself, doll. I'll miss you."

I hugged him back, trying hard not to lose it in front of everyone. "I'll miss you too."

Lowering my voice so that only he could hear, I added, "Take care of him."

"I always do." He let me go and ruffled my hair like the big brother he had always been to me.

I turned to leave through the door, finally face to face with Shyam. He wore shades even though we were still inside of the house. I was sure they were mostly to hide his true emotions from me. His hands were in his pockets as he studied my face from the safety of his sunglasses.

Without saying anything, he walked to the car. I followed behind him. He opened the passenger side for me before moving to the driver's seat. A blacked-out SUV was parked behind his car, ready with his security team to follow us to the private plane.

After we fastened our seatbelts, he drove out of the big gates of his estate. We rode in silence except for the sound of the car shifting gears. I didn't know where to look in the awkwardness that blanketed us. I turned my head to stare out of the passenger window.

Lush, green farmlands surrounded the road. Men and women worked their fields, probably just going about their daily routine. Were any of them experiencing the same heartache that I was right now? Were they using their work to numb their pain? Did they succumb to tears at night when the work was done, and they were alone in their beds?

Yet another tear escaped from the corner of my eye. I hated myself for crying so much. Embarrassed, I swiped my finger quickly to dry it before Shyam saw. I should have known better because nothing I did ever escaped his notice. His hand grabbed mine and squeezed it firmly in his. He rested our joined hands on his lap as he drove on.

The small private airport came into view and my heart dropped in my chest. He parked the car on the tarmac near the only plane in sight. I moved to open my door, but he pulled me to face him before I could. I stared into his sunglasses, seeing my sullen reflection. I moved my hands to the frames and lifted them off his face. Red, puffy eyes stared back at me, wet with tears, just like mine. My fingers trailed along his skin, studying his face—committing every detail to memory. I moved into him and pressed a soft kiss to his lips. His fingers weaved into my hair, holding me close to him one last time.

"I hate you," I whispered as I cried. I didn't understand why he couldn't trust me enough to tell me why I needed to go, but I knew he still wouldn't tell me if I pressed him.

"I know, *jaan*," he said, kissing my cheek. "I'd rather you hate me if it meant you were safe."

He pressed his forehead to mine, holding me close. I inhaled deeply, filling my lungs with his scent so I could store it away for a lifetime.

I said it one last time. "I love you."

"I love you so damn much," he said, looking into my eyes.

With that, he put his sunglasses back on like armor to protect him from the rawness between us. He exited the car and opened the door for me.

He handed my bag over to one of the bodyguards who would be accompanying me on the flight.

I swallowed the lump in my throat and took my first step toward the plane on shaky legs. Then another, and another, until I made it up the ramp, pausing before entering the vessel.

I turned back to find him leaning against the car with his hands in his pockets, facing me. From the outside, he was the picture of power and strength, but I knew the real man inside. Behind the money, guards, and even the sunglasses, he was just Shyam, the man who would forever be afraid to be truly open and honest with anyone, and most importantly, with himself. He was his own worst enemy.

I turned back around and entered the plane. There was nothing left for me here.

Chapter XXIX

Shyam

The rain pelted the window of my office. Despite being on the thirty-eighth floor, the noise from the storm outside gave me the sense that I was in a fishing boat, being tossed about the waves in the middle of a giant storm at sea. That would have explained the unsettling feeling in my gut and the eerie loneliness I felt in my vessel. *The captain always goes down with the ship.*

I sat in my chair looking out the window, examining how the droplets of water beat against the glass and following the wet trails they left as they slid down the surface. Spring was meant to be a cheerful time; however, it was anything but when the clouds overtook the New York City skies.

I wondered what the weather was like in Seattle. I imagined it was just as gloomy and rainy as the city. Was she staring out her window feeling just as miserable as I was? I hoped not. Was someone else making her smile? I'd kill him, even though she deserved better than what I could give her.

"I see you're in the middle of something." Jai's voice intercepted the same series of thoughts that I had nearly every hour of every day. "I can come back if you're too busy."

Even after all of this, he was still an asshole to me.

I didn't respond, too indifferent to turn my chair around and give him the attention he constantly needed as the younger sibling.

I heard the door click and his footsteps approach my desk. That was the other thing about little brothers—they never knew when they weren't wanted.

The sound of the chair leather depressing under his weight irritated me. Loneliness was the only thing I wanted to keep me company.

He spoke, knowing I would listen to what he had to say even if I didn't want to. "I spoke to Mikhail, my informant. It seems like the brotherhood likes the deal. Everything should be finalized soon."

Good, then they could finally get off my back and leave me in fucking peace. The Russians had demanded a nine-month contingency plan to prove that we were serious about our contract. I was distrustful of everyone, but they took it to a whole new level. They had assumed we'd betray them from the moment we offered the deal. They wanted to pull our strings for months until they were sure it wasn't a trick. But there was no trick. I just wanted Amelia safe and for them to give up their mission to retrieve her for their own musings.

"Is she safe?" I asked, still not looking at him.

"It took some convincing, but they don't believe she's anything more than a really intelligent programmer."

Thank fuck for that. No one would ever know about our relationship. I hadn't contacted her since she left for Seattle, against my own desires. I pulled up her number on my phone every night as I lay in my cold bed, my finger hovering over the phone icon. But I never went through with it. That was how I ended my nights, angry at the invisible wall that separated us—the one that kept her safe, but also made me a broken man. I'd toss my phone aside and roll over angrily, desperate for sleep to take me away from reality. But even in my sleep, her face haunted me. I was about five nights away from needing to be committed to an asylum or drinking myself to death. Knowing she was safe was the only thing that gave me solace.

"What are you doing?" he asked, his tone void of the bullshit he was always spewing.

"What does it look like? Knitting you a scarf," I snapped.

"Shyam, you can't run an empire like this. You're driving yourself mad."

I glared at him to back down. "Mind your own business."

"You are my fucking business. I promised Amelia I'd take care of you, but you have to meet me halfway. This isn't like you. Pathetic and sulky." He slammed his fist on my desk.

"Shut up," I said through gritted teeth, ready to pounce on him.

He raised his index finger to the air. "Admit one thing to me—your head's not in it anymore."

My shoulders sagged in agreement with his assessment.

He was right. I resented the business, this life of drugs, criminals, and money. It had cost me the one thing I really cared about. I despised my family legacy. I would burn down all our factories if that meant I could leave the underworld for good and be with her.

"Then get out," he suggested gently.

He was pissing me off. "It's not that easy," I spat.

"Isn't it? Why does it have to be complicated?"

"Because I have a motherfucking empire to run." I stood up and threw the files off my desk, sending papers scattering everywhere. "You wouldn't know the first thing about running this business. You think it's all parties and strippers. The fame and glory mean nothing. Sacrifice and duty is what keeps this shit running." I was screaming so loud that I could feel the veins on my neck ready to burst.

Jai stayed seated, unimpressed with my tantrum. "And this is how you lead an empire? You're either drinking yourself into a stupor or losing your shit when anyone even looks at you the wrong way. This is what a leader looks like?" he said, motioning toward me with his hand.

I dropped back into my chair, feeling defeated.

Jai stood up, composed, like a parent leaving his screaming child in a corner for a time out. I couldn't bear him looking down at me with such pity for my immaturity, so I turned my head, once again diverting my gaze to the rain outside my windows.

His voice was soothing and full of concern. "You only have to stay onboard until the Brotherhood's contingency plan ends." *Nine months.* "What you do after that is up to you."

The door clicked, signaling that I was once again alone.

The pager on my office phone buzzed. I pressed the button to connect the line to my secretary. "Sorry to disturb you, Mr. Sethi. You have a phone call from the CEO of TrackCloud."

Chapter XXX

Amelia

My nerves were a mess. The waiting room was decorated in shades of light blue and white. The navy sitting chairs offered an air of seriousness to the otherwise fresh and modern décor. Silver pendant lights hung low from the ceiling, offering strategically placed focal points. On the far wall, in a large, super-modern font, was the name of the company: TrackCloud.

My heel tapped against the white oak floor as I shook my leg nervously, waiting for them to call me in. I had just completed the mandatory technical part of the interview where I had to come up with code to solve various problems asked by a member of the programming team. My answers would be graded and a member from the interview committee would be calling me in for the final part: an interview with the board members.

I was sweating under my long-sleeved white blouse and pencil skirt. I had opted for business wear instead of the developer dress code of jeans and sneakers. After three weeks of moping around the house in pajamas and gorging myself on Flamin' Hot Cheetos, I'd needed to wear something that didn't remind me of heartbreak and depression. Mom was so glad to have me home and had treated me delicately for the first two weeks, but then my sulking started to get on her nerves. She wasn't impressed that her educated daughter was wasting away in her room, listening to emo songs and checking her cellphone every five minutes for messages. I pressed the SMS button so often that the damn thing froze up on me, as if trying to tell me to "calm the fuck down."

To be honest, I was fortunate to be back in Seattle, but I had little time to enjoy it. I stepped off the plane from India and nearly collapsed into my mother's arms when I got home. I couldn't tell her the whole story, just a brief thing about Shyam and I breaking up because of "differences." She knew there was more to the story but didn't press me for more information. She let me grieve, giving me my space. Then one day, she came into my room and told me to get up and find a job. I was pissed at her for ruining my misery-party-for-one, but she was right. I couldn't spend my life pining away for a man who could easily throw me away without even telling me why. I needed a purpose, and a job would provide me with one.

The first day I arrived in Seattle, I thought he'd at least message me to make sure my flight was okay. No text. Then the second day, I was sure he'd check on me to see if I had settled in at home. Still nothing. On the third day, I was certain he'd reach out to say he missed me as much as I missed him. Absolutely nothing. I obsessed over my need to talk to him, which made me hate myself more than I hated him for ending us. The self-loathing was the worst part. It was one thing for a man to break up with you, but to let him break you to the point of no return was pathetic. And I was the most pathetic woman of them all. That was when Mom stepped in and kicked my ass in a way only a mother could.

Apparently, she had even called Natalie out of desperation to save me from my depression. Nat had packed up all my stuff from my New York apartment and shipped everything over for me. She was also the reason I had landed this interview. One of the recruiters at TrackCloud had been in her graduating class at Caltech. She had referred me to him, and he'd called me immediately for a pre-interview over the phone.

TrackCloud was a startup that collected data to tailor social media to its user. They employed around five hundred employees and were responsible for making location check-ins and photo tagging easier. The algorithms they used were very cutting edge and the field was right up my alley. For the first time in weeks, I was excited about something and it had nothing to do with a guy. This was all for me.

"Ms. Becker." A woman in a smart suit and dark-framed glasses stood in front of the waiting area. "They're ready for you."

I stood up, pressing my hands down my outfit to smooth out the wrinkles and followed her to the boardroom.

"Please come in, Ms. Becker," a man in his mid-forties said. He had a full head of salt-and-pepper hair and sat straight up with the confidence of an industry veteran. *This guy must know his shit.* He sat at the head of the conference table. All six seats on either side of the table were taken by the board, who would also be interviewing me.

I wasn't sure if I was supposed to walk around the table and shake everyone's hand first or just sit down.

The man motioned for me to sit, so I chose the latter. My hands were clammy anyway so I wouldn't have set a good impression leaving streaks of sweat on their hands.

The only seat available was at the other end of the conference table. I pulled out the chair and sat down.

"Thank you for coming in today, Ms. Becker. My name is Brian Howard." He was the CEO. I remembered his name from my research of the company.

He went around the table and introduced me to the rest of the panel. There were three women present, which I found impressive for a tech company.

They grilled me for forty-five minutes on everything from my team-building skills to my past work experience. I tried hard to focus on their questions and not let my mind stray when they asked about my time at Sethi Tech. Flashes of Shyam's face played in my mind before I pushed them out of view and resumed answering questions. I tried to keep my answers technical and void of emotion.

The interview finally ended. "Well, Ms. Becker. It looks like we've covered all the ground that we needed to. We usually take around two to three days to contact interviewees with our decision, but—"

Mr. Howard looked around the table at his colleagues, who were all smiling eagerly. "We'd like to offer you the position of Vice President of Product Development."

I must have heard incorrectly. *Vice President, as in an "executive member"?* I sat frozen in my seat, unsure of how to navigate this mix-up. "I'm sorry, but there's been a mistake. I thought this interview was for the Senior Developer position?" I glanced nervously from smiling face to smiling face around the table. No one mirrored my confusion.

"We're still in need of a candidate for that position, but we feel with your qualifications and skills, you'd be a better fit for the role of Vice President."

"Forgive me, but I wasn't expecting to be considered for that position. When I researched your company, I saw that you currently have a VP of Development."

One of the women at the table, with short gray hair and crystal blue eyes, raised her hand. "That'd be me, Ms. Becker. Unfortunately, I will be retiring in a couple of months and we haven't found anyone qualified enough to take over my position—until *you* applied. You would, of course, train under me until I formally leave so I can answer any questions you might have."

I was floored. This would mean that I would be running the entire developmental side of the company. I was about to vomit. Why the fuck did I eat all those Cheetos this morning?

I didn't know what to say. "Um—thank you."

The woman studied my face. "Are you unhappy with our offer? Of course, we would have to send you an official offer letter with your benefits and stock options outlined, but we thought you'd be happy to hear of our decision beforehand."

"No. That's not it. I'm just in disbelief. It's not every day a twenty-something programmer is asked to be Vice President of a company."

The room erupted in chuckles. "I suppose not," Mr. Howard said. "However, we were thoroughly impressed with your resumé and background. Both of your past employers had only positive things to say about you when I spoke to them over the phone."

My brows furrowed. I hadn't submitted the letter of recommendation that Shyam wrote for me. It felt wrong using it after things ended the way they had. *But, shit!* He had spoken with Shyam? About me? I needed details. Now! *Focus, Becker. Act professional.*

"Oh," I replied, trying to act nonchalant.

"Mr. Sethi was very complimentary of your abilities. He was able to send over some drafts of your code that you wrote while working for him, of course removing confidential information owned by Sethi Tech. We reviewed everything to get an idea of your skill level and we were impressed. Programmers as young as you don't put out code as technically advanced as yours. You should be proud of yourself."

My jaw couldn't move to speak. Shyam had done that for me? Tech companies never shared code like that, especially for employees who'd left the company. But it was the best way for

263

a new employer to see how a person solved programming problems. These technical exams were just filled with riddles that anyone who studied hard enough could solve. However, actual code from actual projects was valuable. Jai had to have been involved too to be able to remove any trace of the shady things I had implemented for them in my code.

I had so many questions, but none of them mattered right now. "Thank you. I accept."

***

After an evening of celebratory cake and champagne with Mom and some friends, I decided to call it a night and head to bed.

I turned off the lights and tucked myself under my oversized comforter with constellations and planets on it. It wasn't very fitting for the new VP of a company, and I should probably invest in something more mature. *Nah. Star Trek, forever!*

Today was the first day in a long time that I had smiled. I was happy, but something kept nagging at me. It was the part of me that wanted to relive the past, even if just for a minute.

I grabbed my phone and scrolled through my messages. My New York friends had texted me their congratulations. I had called Nat as soon as I left the interview and screamed into the phone while she did the same.

I scrolled through my contacts, my fingers moving on their own, making my way to the S section.

His name was the first one listed. I pressed it with out thinking, bringing up his contact information. I hesitated for a split second before pressing the phone icon.

It was too late now to change my mind, so I pressed the phone to my ear. The first ring twisted my stomach into knots, while also giving me relief that my call hadn't been answered yet. The contradicting feelings soon ended before the second ring never sounded.

He answered. I could hear his breathing on the other line. The pounding of my heart stilled to better hear the familiar rhythm of his inhales and exhales.

"Jaan." I closed my eyes to shut off my sense of sight so my brain could focus on the sound that reverberated through phone. His voice still carried the same rich smoothness I remembered.

"Shyam," I choked out.

"Are you okay?" he asked quickly.

"Yes," I lied even though I was so close to falling apart.

He paused before speaking, as if knowing I had just lied to him. "Are you happy?" he asked.

He knew my answer, so I didn't bother indulging him. "Are you?"

Silence.

I redirected the conversation. "Thank you—um—for what you did with TrackCloud." This was the reason I had called in the first place, right?

"You deserve the position. They made the right decision." Hearing him compliment me made my heart soar. He had always been so supportive of my career. "When do you start?"

"In a week. I train under the current Vice President until I take over in about two months."

"I'm proud of you." I could hear his smile through the phone.

I grinned goofily in response. "Thanks. How are things at Sethi Tech?"

"The same. More acquisitions. Jai driving me up the wall."

I chuckled.

His voice grew quiet. "I missed that sound."

The pain resurfaced. I remembered why I had stopped laughing in the first place. It was because of him. Nothing had changed. He still didn't trust me enough to share everything with me. His first response was always to push me away instead of letting me decide my own fate. I couldn't live with someone who's first choice was to run.

"I should go," I said, trying to end the call before I burst into tears.

He sighed. "*Jaan.* I wish I could tell you everything. You have to trust that what I did was only to protect you."

I lost my temper. "And you should trust me enough to let me decide what's best for me. Take care of yourself, Shyam."

He let out a bigger exhale than before, signaling his loss of will to fight with me again. "Goodbye, *jaan.*" His voice sounded defeated.

And just like that, I revisited the nights of crying into my pillow until I fell asleep.

CHAPTER XXXI

AMELIA

10 months later

"…and with the new features implemented in the recognition application, we can expect our social media clients to increase their match accuracies to a level of 99.99 percent accuracy."

"So, there's a 0.001 percent chance that there could be a miss?" Andrew, the VP of Marketing asked trying to throw me off my game with his sarcasm.

I plastered on my most professional smile and leaned one hip against the wall next to the projection monitor that displayed the statistics I had organized into the presentation for today. I crossed one leg over the other and did the same with my arms over my chest, standing with my spine long and an air of coolness as I looked down at him in his seat. His hair was usually perfectly coifed on his head and shiny from tons of product, but today his head looked like it had gotten into a fight with a weed-whacker. "That small percentage only accounts for human manipulation, like getting plastic surgery or...a bad haircut." My voice was even and lacked any apparent hint of sarcasm, even though my meaning was laced in it.

The entire room caught on and chuckled as Andrew shifted uncomfortably in his seat. It wasn't the nicest thing to say, but that man had been out to undermine me since I started at TrackCloud nearly fifteen months ago. At first, I was quiet and let him make his snide remarks, not having enough courage for retaliation. However, I quickly learned that wasn't how to handle jerks like that. It was better to put them in their place.

He had been with the company for about three years now, so he wasn't a total idiot, but the tech side was my domain. His job was to market whatever my departments made, and he needed to remember that. He wasn't my superior in the hierarchy of the company, though he felt he was because of the small thing he carried between his legs. I say "small" because it probably was, from the way he had been trying to prove himself by dumping on my work every chance he got.

I continued, assuming he would shut up long enough to let me wrap up without interrupting. "Our next step is to draft roll-out schedules for each of our clients. Facebook is anticipating to fully integrate the feature in six weeks, while Twitter has asked for a four-week time frame."

I took about fifteen minutes worth of questions from the group before thanking everyone for their time and offering a promise to have notes emailed out from my assistant in the next hour. Colleagues approached me on their way out of the boardroom, excitedly discussing the new feature and congratulating me on a job well done—everyone except Andrew. However, that didn't ruin my mood. It always felt great wrapping up a project that the company was excited about.

I collected my leather portfolio and phone and made my way to my office. My black patent-leather heels clicked against the floor as I strode down the hall. I had to hurry back to finish up reading through some product reports before my next meeting, which would keep me occupied until after lunchtime. I hated when my assistant booked me through lunch, but it must have been important to keep me from eating. I liked to visit the taco truck next to the building during my lunch hour. *Old habits die hard.*

Once in my office, I shut the door and kicked off my heels. I still preferred flats, but heels were growing on me. I unbuttoned my white suit jacket before dropping into my ergonomically designed chair. I wore a black lace shell underneath that was a touch too saucy for the office, but it hugged my curves in all the right places, leaving a smooth appearance under my jacket. I sat cross-legged in my chair with my feet tucked up under my legs. Luckily, my tailored trousers had some give in the seam so I could fold myself comfortably in my chair.

I unlocked my computer and loaded my documents for review. My assistant, Lucy, was a sweet older lady who had only been hired in the last month or so. She took care of me like a daughter, making sure I had an unlimited supply of beverages and snacks in my office. Every morning, she had a hot cup of spiced chai waiting for me on my desk. The only thing that sucked about her was her scheduling skills; I needed to review that with her, but it'd have to wait until tomorrow because today was too busy.

I was happy at my job. I finally felt like I found my "sweet job"—the one you stay at for at least five years. I had the respect of my superiors and often worked closely with the CEO to pitch product ideas or change the courses of current projects.

On the personal front, I still lived at home with Mom. She was able to cut back on her hours while I supported the both of us with my salary. I had even reconnected with a lot of my childhood friends and went out with them sometimes. Though, lately, I rarely had time to do that since I was putting in extra hours at work. Being a VP wasn't a nine-to-five job. Most days,

I was the last to leave the office. It was pretty much the janitor and me left in the building, working into the night.

I took a sip from my steaming mug of chai. It was good, but never as good as the ones I had in India when I was with—

A knock sounded at my door. Lucy rarely used the pager button on the phone to let me know when she needed to talk to me. *Another thing to add to the list of things to review tomorrow.* I shoved my feet back into my heels that I had hidden under my desk. "Come in."

Lucy popped her head inside. "Your eleven o'clock is here."

Already? I glanced at the time. *Shit.* What was the company I was meeting with again? S.S. Inc.? I had forgotten to research them since I'd been busy prepping for my big meeting earlier this morning.

I stood up and buttoned up my jacket and smoothed out the wrinkles from my pants. "Right. Send them in," I said while looking down to avoid tripping as I rounded my desk to greet my next appointment.

The person halted just inside the office door. I looked up with my well-rehearsed professional smile fixed on my face, prepared to offer a handshake. I froze when I caught sight of who it was, and my smile vanished. I stared in shock at my visitor.

He took my hand in his, squeezing it gently, setting my skin on fire—the same effect he had always had on me. "Ms. Becker.

How are you?" After all this time, his deep voice still brought my insides to life.

"Shyam," I whispered. Breath had left my lungs and I felt nearly ready to pass out from being so close to him.

I looked over at Lucy, my eyes wide with panic. *"Wow,"* she mouthed, grinning like a schoolgirl, before shutting the door and leaving me alone with the man who haunted my thoughts every day and left me wet in my dreams every night.

"You look well, Amelia." A sly grin spread across his lips as he looked me up and down, taking in my figure in the suit.

His eyes burned me. I pulled my hand from his and wiped my palm on the side of my pants to ease the discomfort in my flesh, singed from his touch.

"Why are you here?" I asked quietly.

"I have a business proposition I'd like to discuss. May I sit down?" He motioned to the chair in front of my desk.

"Of course," I answered nervously. I moved around the desk on shaky legs, somehow managing to sit down in my chair without stumbling.

He looked around my office, sizing it up. I had opted to decorate in blacks, silvers, and whites because I preferred a sleeker sci-fi vibe. It made me feel more comfortable, like I was coding in my bedroom at home. "You've done well. This office suits your style, *jaan*."

His nickname for me snapped me out my reverie. "What are you doing here, Shyam?"

A knowing smile spread to his face. "I have an executive position at Sethi Tech that I need to fill."

I saw through his motives. He was playing at something. "I'm not sure that we have anyone from the board looking to leave anytime soon."

"Once you hear the offer, I'm sure you'll be able to find someone for the role." His tone was mischievous which could only mean trouble for me.

I was losing my cool, and he was loving that he could still get a rise out of me. "This really isn't in my job description. Maybe I could have one of the recruiters meet with you instead." I stood up, ready to leave. I refused to let him see me break, and I would if I sat there across from him any longer.

"Sit down, Amelia," he said. His tone was clipped.

I refused to take orders from him again. "I prefer to stand."

He got to the point, realizing he was losing me fast. "I'm in need of a new Chief Technical Officer."

"You have Jai as your CTO. Why do you need a new one?" I asked, utterly confused.

"He's left the company."

"What? When?" His brother had always been by his side, so why not now?

He clasped his hands in front of his chest, elbows resting on the arms of the chair. "It was a recent change. I'm in the process of reorganizing the company."

"Are you two fighting or something?" It wasn't unheard of, these brothers bickering, but for Jai to leave the company was serious.

"No, nothing like that. The split was amicable. He's pursuing *other* endeavors."

"Like…?" I asked with my hands on my hips waiting for an explanation. His brief answers were pissing me off.

He paused for a moment before answering. "The family business needed a new leader."

This made no sense. Shyam oversaw their cartel empire. "What happened to the—um—old leader?"

He shifted to rest his ankle on his knee, as if this were just a casual conversation. "He decided it was time to retire."

My eyebrow hitched with skepticism. The family business was his life. He did everything he could to preserve it. Whatever his reason was, though, it was no longer any of my business. I chose to not press any further for information.

"So, Jai no longer works for Sethi Tech and you want someone from my company to fill his role?" Tough chance that I was going to give up anybody from my team to work for another company.

"I have someone in particular in mind." The glint in his hazel eyes shined brighter as his stare focused on me.

I stared blankly back at him, waiting for him to name a colleague that he was interested in. He didn't say anything, just sat there staring at me with his intense gaze, void of any humor.

Suddenly, it clicked. I gaped at him. "Wait. You mean me?" I raised my voice in surprise and pointed to my chest.

He stared back at me, confirming my assumptions.

He had to be crazy to show up here as if nothing ever happened, assuming I'd just drop everything to do whatever he asked of me, like the last time he asked me to work for him. "I already have a job!"

"I realize that. This would be a promotion from your current position," he said, his eyes trained on me.

"Let me guess, I'd be working under *you* as CTO?" I shot back, unaware of the innuendo I had laid out for him.

He took it and ran. "Only if you wanted to work *under* the CEO."

I lost it. "This isn't fair. You can't just show up here with your suggestive comments and charming smile and get me to do whatever you want. This is *my* life now, and you don't get to just snap your finger and get me to uproot everything I've worked so hard for just to suit your whims." I broke down in tears.

He stood up, moving to round the desk, but I stopped him before he could touch me. "No. Don't." I stood holding myself for comfort, but it wasn't the same. Five minutes with him and my soul already craved him for peace. I had spent the past year trying to rid myself of my need for him, and I couldn't go back just because he had shown up here playing games with me.

He watched me, looking defeated. "Am I too late?" he asked quietly.

I closed my eyes, already pained by what I was about to say. "Yes."

His shoulders fell as if I had just told him today was his last day of life.

Hesitantly, he pulled out a hotel keycard from his pocket. "Meet me tonight, at my hotel room."

I didn't move from my spot. If I took him up on his invitation, I wouldn't be able to resist his hold over me in the privacy of a hotel room. At least I was at work, with lots of people just outside of my door. I was strong but not strong enough to shield my heart from him in private.

He placed the card on my desk when I didn't take it from him. "I was hoping it wasn't too late, but I'd still like to explain everything to you. I'll be in town until tomorrow morning." He left the office without giving me a second glance.

My hands balled up into fists as I pressed them into my stomach. I was going to throw up. I looked over to the key on my desk, teasing me with the hotel name and room number in large black print, obnoxiously reminding me how weak I was because I wanted to use it.

I quickly chucked the damn thing into the wastebin next to my desk. The letters on the card still shone brightly, like little neon lights amidst the rubbish of papers in the container. I dug it out of the bin and twiddled it in my fingers, feeling its weight rest heavily on me in more ways than one.

Pocketing the card, I grabbed my phone and my bag and headed out of the office. I needed air.

I bolted down the street, walking several blocks away so I could be away from anyone I might run into from work who happened to be heading out for lunch. Small talk wasn't on my agenda right now. I needed to have a "big" talk.

I found a spot outside of the library nearby and took a seat on the steps. I scrolled through my phone, looking for the contact information of the only person who could understand the complicated man who had just waltzed back into my life.

"Hi, doll. Long time, no hear." Jai's smooth and easy-going tone provided me with the sibling comfort I desperately needed right now.

I smiled into the phone, glad to hear his cheerful voice. "Hi, Jai. How are you?"

"Probably better than you. I assume if you're calling me, then my brother paid you a visit?"

I sighed heavily into the phone. "You assume correctly."

"By the way, he told me about your new job. Congratulations, boss lady."

"I should be congratulating you, *boss man*." I was still surprised that Jai had taken over the Sethi empire. He was more than capable of running it, but his brother was the one who had considered it his life's mission.

"Ah, it's nothing. It's a dirty job, but someone's gotta do it," he said, as if running the biggest drug cartel in the world was no big deal. "Shyam try to convince you to take over as CTO?"

I was sure he knew of his brother's motives for coming to New York, so I didn't have to explain any of it to him. "Among other things."

Jai sucked in a breath over the line. "I think you should give him a chance. You don't understand what he went through these past months."

The anger started to rise in me again. "How about what I went through?" I raised my voice in frustration, causing passers-by to look over at me with more interest than I needed right now.

"He didn't have much of a choice. He had to send you away."

"Why?" I demanded.

His voice was quiet to counter my heated emotions. "You should let him explain it to you. It's not my place."

"No. I'm fed up with everyone keeping things from me. Both of you treat me like I'm a fragile doll who can't handle anything. Neither of you went through the shit I went through in India and survived to talk about it."

"Amelia, we were desperate." His tone indicated that I needed to hear him out. "Tarun was involved in some deep shit when he took you." His voice had grown quieter, probably to avoid anyone overhearing him.

"Like what?"

"Human trafficking. He was planning to sell you to the Russian mafia."

My gut churned and I let out an audible gasp.

"And when Tarun died, they still wanted what was promised to them. The Brotherhood don't let things like death terminate contracts that were made with them. They're some twisted-ass motherfuckers who make me look like a saint."

Oh God, all this time, I'd had a bounty over my head, and I didn't even know. Was it safe now? Was Mom safe? My heart stopped, thinking that someone could kidnap her at any moment. "Are they still after me?" I asked, panic rising in my voice.

"No. We struck a deal with them. They wanted to make sure we were good on our word for nine months before dropping the outstanding deal."

Relief took hold of me.

"But do you get why Shyam had to send you away? You were safer away from him. If they had known he cared for you, you'd had a bigger target on your head."

God, I had been oblivious to the stress he had been experiencing since I left, while I was free to live my life without looking over shoulder every day. He was the one who was doing it for me.

"Why didn't anyone tell me?" I was frustrated that they had kept this from me. I should have been the first person to know.

"And have you live out the rest of your life in fear? Would you have been able to sleep or leave your house if you knew that there were men out there planning to whore you out in exchange for money?" My gut twisted from the seriousness of Jai's tone. He had a point.

"Even if you couldn't be with him, he wanted you to have a chance at happiness. And look at how you've thrived in Seattle."

Shyam had done all of this for me. He always said he couldn't tell me because it wasn't safe, but I just thought he didn't trust me to make the right decision. This must really have been the only way to throw them off my scent.

"Did you have men keeping an eye on me this whole time?" I already knew the answer, but I asked anyway.

He chuckled. "You obviously still don't know how the Sethi's operate if you have to ask that question."

I smiled. *Control Freaks.*

Jai continued, "He still loves you. He never stopped. He was a goddamn mess after you left. His heart wasn't in the family busines anymore because you took it with you. That's why he left the business—so if you gave him a second chance, you'd never be in danger again because he left that world."

My heart squeezed in my chest. This fucking man. "Jai. I have to go."

He chuckled again. "I'll see ya later, doll. And I mean that."

I pulled out the snake necklace that I still carried in my purse everywhere I went but hadn't had the courage to wear again. I clasped it around my neck with shaky fingers, then abandoned my heels and bolted through the streets, weaving in and out of pedestrians and bikers. I ran so fast that I was sure my feet would be covered in filth and have blisters later, but I didn't care. Adrenaline and need fueled my sprint.

The ten-minute run felt like hours. The ride up the elevator from the lobby felt like years. The dash to the hotel-suite door felt like a lifetime. The wait for the light on the key reader to turn green nearly killed me.

I turned the knob and pushed through the door, unsure of what I'd say or do when I met him face to face again. I struggled to steady my breath from the run—or nerves.

The room was dark and the drapes were pulled shut. The sitting room of the suite was empty. Maybe he had already left? Was it me who was too late?

I walked further inside, calling out for him, "Shyam?"

The bedroom door was open. My heart prayed that he was still in there.

I walked through it. Lit candles were everywhere.

And there he was, standing with his hands in his pockets and a knowing smile on his face.

I couldn't think of how to start so I settled on, "Hey."

"Hey," he replied, unmoving. He eyed my bare feet. "Where are your shoes?"

I ignored his question and stepped closer to him. "I talked to Jai."

He didn't seem surprised. "I know."

My heart was beating out of my chest, making it difficult to speak more than a few words at a time. "He told me every-thing."

He moved closer to me. "I know."

I grabbed onto the front of his shirt, clutching tightly as I shook him. "You should have told me," I gritted out.

His hands flew to my arms, gently calming me. He shook his head out in disappoint of himself. "I know."

284

I studied his face, seeing honesty and heartbreak written all over it. For the first time, I could see him clearly—no walls or armor.

"I accept."

His eyebrow knitted as he questioned my meaning with his gaze.

"The job offer. I accept," I answered hastily not wanting to waste another minute without laying my cards on the table.

He grinned. "It comes with strings, *jaan*."

There was always a catch with him. "Like what?"

He pulled out a little red box from his pocket. Bending down onto one knee, he opened it revealing its glittering contents—a ring with the biggest diamond I had ever seen. "That you're mine. Forever."

Tears flooded my eyes as I watched the most powerful man I knew, on his knees, begging me to be his. I nodded, unable to speak.

He slipped the ring onto my finger. It sparkled as the candlelight hit it in all the right spots.

I knelt to meet him and burrowed myself into his body, needing to be close to the man that I had missed for far too long.

"Never push me away again," I whispered, smiling into his chest as he rested his chin on my head.

"Never."

EPILOGUE

SHYAM

6 Years Later

The sun had just set, leaving my office shadowed in the mild darkness that comes with dusk. With every sunset in December, the Indian sun took its heat with it when it slept for the night, allowing a chill to permeate every room in the house.

The light from my desk lamp kept me company as I wrapped up paperwork in my office. I attempted to not make work a habit whenever I was on winter vacation in India, but my duties at Sethi Tech needed attention. We had acquired several more startups in the past few months and I needed to give the contracts one last look over before signing them to make the mergers complete.

Through my open office door, I heard a loud crash down the hallway. My heartbeat quickened as I pushed back from my desk. My stride was usually long but each step I took now was the size of two of my regular steps. I could have sworn the sound had come from the library.

The door was cracked, but I couldn't see in clearly. I pushed the door in slowly, my body on high alert. I peered into the darkness and saw several books scattered onto the floor and two small figures in front of one of the bookcases.

"I don't see it!" whispered one of the figures, who was on her tiptoes, trying to see on a shelf that was too high for her.

"Maybe it's not here," whispered the voice of the littlest figure.

"Mommy put it back here yesterday. I saw her," the girl scolded the little boy, who stood behind her, watching her expectantly.

The boy tried to keep his voice quiet, but it came out a shout. "Hurry up, before—"

I flicked on the light switch, bathing the room in bright lights. The two little figures were startled. The girl backed away from the bookcase and the boy hid his hands behind his back, face frozen with guilt. They both stared up at me with doe eyes like I had just caught them in the middle of committing the most heinous crime—as heinous as a five- and three-year-old could commit.

"What are you two doing down here?" I asked, trying hard to hide my grin. Why did kids look so damn cute when they were caught red-handed? Maybe I was just a pushover for them when they misbehaved. For that reason, their mother was the disciplinarian.

"We were looking for a book," said Meena. Even though she was only five and dressed in a pink night dress with ruffles, she carried herself with the air of a woman. She looked like her mother, with green eyes and freckled cheeks, and was smart like her too, but her hair was dark like mine and she had my stubbornness.

"Well, you're in the right place," I said, eyeing the puddle of books around their bare feet. "What book are you looking for?"

"The one we read last night," Dylan exclaimed as he jumped up and down in his striped pajamas. He was only three years old and was the cutest boy I had ever seen, with his mop of black hair and chubby cheeks. He could never stay still and was always on the go. He was just like me, always looking for something new to explore.

"*Rikki-Tikki-Tavi*?" It was the only book they ever wanted to read since landing here for Christmas vacation.

"Yeaaaaaaaaaaah!" they shouted, both jumping up and down now.

I remembered I had left the book on the coffee table, so I turned around and grabbed it. "Here it is," I said, shaking it in the air.

"Yayyyyyy!" Finding the book earned me a round of applause from my audience.

"Now, let's clean up these books on the floor and go find Mom. You two should be in bed by now."

After we cleaned up all the books, we made our way upstairs to their room. They had separate bedrooms at our house in New York, but Dylan needed to sleep with Meena here in India, or else he'd end up in our bed in the middle of the night. I refused to let that be an option because I wanted his mom to myself.

With the book tucked under my arm, I held two little hands in my oversized ones as we walked down the hall. The walls had once been covered with art pieces, but now they were filled with family photos. We passed our wedding photos, which had been taken here in India.

We had a traditional Indian wedding here at the house shortly after I proposed. I couldn't wait any longer to make her my wife. The entire house staff were thrilled to host the event for us and went to great lengths to make her dream wedding come to life. All my men were in attendance, as well as her mother and friends from Seattle and New York. She was a vision in her bridal wear, adorned with jewels and the finest fabrics. I had never seen a woman so beautiful.

We passed photos of when Meena and Dylan were born and their first Christmases here in the house. Family photos with Jai, Zayn, and her mother were included in our photo gallery, too.

We entered their room, and the kids barreled toward their mother, who was reclining on the bed, waiting for them to come back.

"Where were you, kiddos? I thought you were just going to go pick out a book, not take a mini vacation downstairs!" my wife said, her eyes alight with happiness as she cuddled a child in each arm. *My wife.* I always knew Amelia was the most radiant woman I had ever laid eyes on, but after becoming a mother, she had a glow about her that was undeniable. She had taken to motherhood like it was second nature to her.

It was just like her. She was great at anything she tried. She had taken up my offer to be CTO of Sethi Tech and transformed the company. We no longer meddled in illegal business but took a new direction under her guidance. It was her idea to use our expertise in tracking software to help locate women and children who had been abducted for various purposes like human trafficking.

I was still the CEO of the company, but she handled it like she was the boss. She pretty much *was* the boss. She made it a point to hire more women in the company to increase diversity. She took the reigns and did an even better job than Jai had when he worked there, in my opinion. And I found her way less annoying than my brother.

Jai was happy in his new role as head of the Sethi family business. He had been busy lately, flying from one country to another maintaining order and growing the business. Right now, he was in Russia doing God knows what with God knows who. He would still confide certain things about the business in me, but for the most part, I stayed out of his dealings. It was no longer my place to participate. The entire underworld knew I was out of the game and that Jai was in charge, allowing me to live out the rest of my days in well-deserved peace.

"Are you coming, Daddy?" Dylan asked impatiently as I stood in the doorway.

I strolled to the bed with the book in my hand and passed it to Amelia, giving her a tender kiss on her lips. She hummed a sweet sound against my lips before opening the book. "Where did we leave off yesterday?"

I snuggled into the bed next to my family. Meena pushed herself onto my lap and swung an arm around my neck as she peered at the book, her long hair brushing against my chin.

"The part where the cobra is going to attack the family and the mongoose is coming to rescue them."

"Oh, right," Amelia said, turning the pages to get to the right page.

"I think the snake is going to win!" exclaimed Dylan from his spot on Amelia's lap, as if the ending would have changed after reading this book for the fiftieth time.

"Me too," Meena agreed. "Snakes are fast and can bite skin so hard until you die!" I should have been more worried with how she relished in pain and death. I'd need to keep one eye on her when she was older. The need for destruction obviously ran deep in her blood just like it did in mine.

"Who do you think will win, Daddy?" Dylan asked, his eyes wide and ready to hang on my every word as he always did when I spoke.

I glanced at Amelia, who was smiling at me with an expression so full of love. My heart was complete because of her. I grinned back at her sensing she already knew my answer. "The mongoose always wins."

THE END

Not ready to say goodbye to the Sethi Brothers just yet?

Turn the page to see a sneak peak of Jai's story.

Prologue

Jai

I hated Russia. It was cold. It was dreary. And the people I had to meet with were intolerable. I could get along with the most withdrawn and difficult of personalities—my brother was proof of that. But the Brotherhood was the most disagreeable organization I had been forced to deal with. It had a history of having members with the most combative personalities, but lately it had only gotten worse.

Shyam and I had built a relationship with the former leader. Granted, it hadn't been a perfect relationship, because the Russians weren't ones to have amicable relationships with anyone. But the relationship had been clear. Boundaries had been obvious, and roles defined. However, with new leadership came new rules—many of which I wouldn't abide by.

The heels of an army of snow boots belonging to my men slapped against the uneven rock bed of the cave. The pathway was narrow, cluttered with mounded stalagmites growing from the ground. I did my best to duck my head to avoid being impaled by protruding rock as I walked. The only light we had to guide us was the fire from the torch that one of my men carried. The eeriness of the tunnel was the only reprieve from the unforgiving blizzard outside. This was why I had dreaded coming here. Both options for meeting place were equally abysmal.

My jaw tightened upon seeing the stocky figure of the conniving tyrant as I approached him. Everything about him looked foul. His hair was a sandy-blond color that didn't look clean and the unkempt scruff on his face only added to his dirty appearance. The only feature that looked clear and somewhat pure were his eyes—they were the brightest shade of green. Too bad he even managed to make his best feature appear maniacal with the way his eyelids squinted, as if he were in the middle of planning out his next sinister move.

The gold from the fillings in his mouth glinted in the firelight, making his devious smile difficult to miss. His band of equally diabolical brothers surrounded him, just looking for any excuse to draw blood. His ogre of a cousin and right-hand man, Igor, stood closest to him, whispering something in his ear that elicited a gut-curdling chuckle.

Leonid Petrov, head of the Russian Brotherhood. He had earned that title in the most dishonorable of ways.

"Leonid." I nodded, coming to a stop with my own men flanking my sides. Everyone was packing ammo, but that was standard procedure when doing any sort of business with the Brotherhood. Guns were always involved.

He stared me down, staying still as he sized us up. In one quick move, he invaded my space, grabbing my hand. My men reacted quickly and drew their guns, aiming them at him. In response, his men did the same to us.

He rested his chest against my frame and grabbed my shoulder with his free hand, pulling me in closer. "Welcome back, brother," he said as if we were old friends and he was giving me a hug, but I knew better. He was instigating shit, praying for a fight.

I pulled away from him, revolted by his proximity.

"There's no need for weapons with family," he warned, eyeing the barricade of rifles before him.

"Cut the shit, Leonid." If he thought I would back down, he was wrong.

The corner of one side of his mouth perked up into a crooked smile.

From my periphery, I could see my informant, Mikhail. He was my inside window to the ongoings of the Brotherhood. My eyes never fully flicked to him to avoid drawing attention to any semblance of recognition. Leonid's eyes were already hungry—hungry for any reason kill.

"I want my money." The force of my voice caused it to echo off the walls of the cave, invading listening ears from all corners. I had delivered my services to him, supplying enough product for distribution and for his own personal whims, but hadn't received payment for my last shipment, over a month ago.

His gaze fell to his feet as he chuckled to himself, as if laughing at some joke only he could hear. His men all followed suit, snickering as if they were in on this imaginary joke too.

His neon eyes snapped back to mine—all humor vanished. "No."

I didn't react to his acerbity, mostly because he yearned for my fear and uncertainty.

My expression remained flat and unreadable. "Then I have no choice but to terminate service."

He scoffed. "No, you won't. We owe you nothing. You stole that bitch from us when she was rightfully ours."

I clenched my fist so tightly against my side that I felt the band of my family ring dig into my flesh at the mention of my sister. "That deal was settled with your last *Pakhan*." *Boss.*

"I am the new *Pakhan* and I see no need to keep my end of deals if you do not do the same," he smirked.

I hadn't been running this empire for so long by giving my product away for free, and I wouldn't start doing it for the likes of scum like Leonid.

I moved in closer, towering over his short frame. "You underestimate me," I said, keeping my voice low so that only he could hear. "You'd do well to keep me happy. I won't be as easy to take down as your father."

His eyes widened at my revelation. He hadn't thought anyone else knew. I almost hadn't figured it out, but unlike the unrightful boss of the Brotherhood, I had access to all secrets in the underworld. My skills at hacking were unmatched, even by the Russians. I was a damned near tech genius, and anything I ever needed to know was at my fingertips, especially those things that I wasn't meant to know.

Leonid was, for once at a loss for words, so I continued speaking for his ears only. "Let's see how your Brothers react to hearing the truth of who really killed their former *Pakhan*. I imagine they won't fare too well finding out they were duped by one of their own." My tone was threatening enough to force him to shuffle backward to evade the knife that was my tongue.

I straightened up and redirected my gaze to the band of Brothers before me. I was certain none of them had heard what had transpired between their boss and me, judging from the puzzled looks on their faces. The only one who looked worried was Igor, which led me to believe that he was just as guilty as Leonid.

I glanced back over to Leonid, who's eyes were now full of bane. Satisfied with the outcome, I nodded to him. *"Dasvidani-ya." Until we meet again.*

I turned to walk away, my back to the Brothers, and my men followed my lead. But before I stepped out of earshot, I turned back to address the eyes that were on me with one last blessing. "Long live your *Pakhan.*"

He wouldn't.

ORDER HERE FOR MORE.

Author's Notes

Thank you for reading *Empowered*. I hope you enjoyed Shyam and Amelia's story as much I enjoyed writing it. I'd love to read your reviews of both *Power* and *Empowered*!

If you need more of the Sethi's, pre-order Jai's story (coming this Spring/Summer) now! I promise you; it will be one hell of a ride.

Also be sure to follow me on Instagram and Goodreads! And visit my website at www.victoriawoods.com to sign up for my mailing list!

First and foremost, I need to thank you, the reader. The fact that you even chose to read this book, makes me all giddy inside! I am enjoying this writing adventure because of readers like you. I love hearing your feedback and seeing you posts on social media. You inspire me to sit down in front of this laptop every day and write.

My writing journey has been one hell of a whirlwind. I'm in awe of all the amazing people I've met along the way.

To my editor, Paisley, thank you for keeping me in check and being the devil's advocate to my thoughts. You keep these characters real and their emotions true. I'm so thankful for your keen eye.

To Cherie, my cover designer, I'm so glad I found you. You are one hell of an artist and you just understand what I want. I'm grateful to have been blessed by your talent.

To the SS, I can't thank you enough for your support. A random chance meeting in this *bookish* world turned into a real friendship that I feel so lucky to have every day. Love you guys!

Lastly, I couldn't do this without my husband. Your love and support inspire me to keep going every day. Love you, boo!